*She was the most gorgeous horse
Melanie had ever seen.*

Even in the dim light of the stall, Melanie could see the perfect line of her back, her arched neck, the swell of her muscled hindquarters, her long legs, and her massive shoulders. Image had balance, beauty, and power.

But what drew Melanie most was the gleam of curiosity in the filly's gaze. Image was studying Melanie just as closely as Melanie was studying her. Melanie caught her breath, amazed at the intelligence that radiated from the filly's eyes.

"Maybe all the grooms think you're a pain, but I think you're perfect," Melanie whispered. "No wonder Fredericka spoils you," she added, lightly caressing the filly's neck. "She knows how special you are, and I bet she loves you lots. I think I might have fallen in love with you, too."

Collect all the books in the Thoroughbred series

THOROUGHBRED Super Editions

ASHLEIGH'S Thoroughbred Collection

*coming soon

THOROUGHBRED

THE BAD LUCK FILLY

CREATED BY
JOANNA CAMPBELL

WRITTEN BY
ALICE LEONHARDT

HarperEntertainment
An Imprint of HarperCollinsPublishers

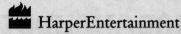 **HarperEntertainment**

An Imprint of HarperCollins*Publishers*

10 East 53rd Street, New York, NY 10022-5299

This is a work of fiction. The characters, incidents, and dialogues are
products of the author's imagination and are not to be construed
as real. Any resemblance to actual events or persons, living
or dead, is entirely coincidental.

 Produced by 17th Street Productions,
an Alloy Online, Inc. company

HarperCollins books are available at special quantity discounts
for bulk purchases for sales promotions, premiums, or fund-raising.
For information, please call or write:
Special Markets Department, HarperCollins Publishers,
10 East 53rd Street, New York, NY 10022-5299.
Telephone: (212) 207-7528. Fax: (212) 207-7222.

ISBN 0-06-105873-4

 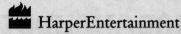
First printing: August 2000

Printed in the United States of America

Visit HarperEntertainment on the World Wide Web at
www.harpercollins.com

❖ 10 9 8 7 6 5 4 3 2 1

1

"MAYBE DECIDING TO EXERCISE-RIDE FOR VINCE JONES WAS a big mistake," sixteen-year-old Melanie Graham told her cousin, Christina Reese. The two girls were walking down the gravel drive that wound through the rows of barns at Turfway Park. It was early in the morning, and except for barn lights, the backside area was dark.

But even at five A.M. the racetrack's backside was teeming with activity. Trainers such as Vince Jones employed dozens of grooms, stable hands, hotwalkers, and exercise riders, and they all started working before the sun came up.

"A mistake!" Christina repeated. Just like Melanie, she carried her exercise saddle and helmet. "Are you crazy? Vince is the best trainer in Kentucky. The best on the East Coast. Probably the best in the whole

1

United States!"

Melanie rolled her eyes. "I don't care if he's the best trainer in the galaxy. He's got more rules than the teachers at school, and he's a big grouch."

"He just likes things his own way," Christina explained. "But you wait. When you ride for him this morning, I bet you'll learn lots."

"I guess," Melanie responded, feeling unconvinced.

When they reached Vince's row of stalls, Melanie looked around. Dozens of gorgeous Thoroughbreds were being fed, walked, groomed, and saddled. The area was spotless, the workers quiet and calm. It was very impressive, and very intimidating.

Christina's right, Melanie corrected herself. She *could* learn a lot from Vince. She just hated someone barking orders at her. Christina had been riding for Vince for several weeks, so she'd adjusted to his gruff ways. Melanie preferred trainers who told her to use her own judgment and let her learn from her mistakes.

Not that there have been that many trainers clamoring for me lately, Melanie thought ruefully. After a bad accident in a race on a colt named Fast Gun, winning had eluded her. Fortunately, Christina's parents, Ashleigh and Mike Reese, owners of Whitebrook Farm, had continued to believe in Melanie. Over the summer she had raced several of Whitebrook's horses. But it wasn't until several weeks ago, after she'd won the Breeder's Futurity on Wonder's Star, one of the farm's top two-year-olds, that Vince Jones had brusquely told Melanie to come exercise-ride for him, too.

And that's what she was doing this morning. Secretly Melanie had to admit that she'd been thrilled when Vince had asked her to ride for him. After he watched her ride, maybe he'd ask her to jockey for him, too.

I'd better ride well, Melanie thought, biting her bottom lip. That wasn't going to be easy, since she had no idea what sort of horses Vince would give her to ride.

A groom walked by leading a handsome bay colt. "Morning, Chris." He nodded at Christina, then glanced at Melanie as if wondering who she was.

Melanie felt a pang of jealousy. This weekend Turfway was holding its big Labor Day weekend races. Christina would be racing Gratis, a colt Vince trained, as well as Wonder's Star. Both were super two-year-olds and possible Kentucky Derby contenders. Christina's name had even been mentioned in several newspapers, and Vince Jones had been quoted as saying, "With jockey Christina Reese on Gratis, the colt has a better-than-average chance of winning." Not exactly glowing praise, but it was about as enthusiastic as Vince ever got.

Melanie sighed. She would be racing several horses at Turfway, too, but none was as outstanding as Gratis or Wonder's Star. Most of them would be hard-pressed to even place in a race, let alone win.

Oh, quit feeling sorry for yourself, Melanie thought as she followed Christina toward the office. She needed to stop telling herself she couldn't win. Ever since she'd come to live with Christina's family at White-brook Farm in Kentucky, she'd dreamed about becoming a jockey. As soon as she had turned sixteen she'd gotten her apprentice jockey's license. Now, just as in her dreams, she'd spent the spring and summer riding and racing as many horses as she could. So what was the problem? Was she just worn out from pushing so hard all summer, trying to prove she could be a *winning* jockey?

"Let's check the schedule to see who we're riding," Christina said when they reached the office. "I hope Vince didn't put me on too many horses. I want to spend some time with Star this morning." Her cousin's expression brightened when she said the big chestnut colt's name. "He clocked great yesterday, did I tell you? He's definitely ready for tomorrow's race."

Hearing the affection in Christina's voice, Melanie felt another pang of jealousy. She thought about Pirate, an ex-racehorse who had gone blind, and Trib, the pony who had taught her how to ride. They were the only horses Melanie had ever felt a bond with—the kind of bond that Christina had with Star. This summer she must have ridden or worked at least a hundred different horses, and many of them were special. But none had been special to *her*. That was what she wanted more than anything—one special horse to love, and to love her back.

The office was empty except for one other exercise

4

rider looking over the schedule.

"Uh-oh, you've got Fortune's Way," Christina said to Melanie when she saw the list.

The other rider chuckled. "Vince puts all the new riders on Yankee."

Melanie looked confused. "Yankee? But I thought you said his name was Fortune."

"We nicknamed him that because he yanks your arms off," Christina explained. Turning, she pulled a protective vest from a hook on the wall and handed it to Melanie.

"What's this for? I'm not planning to fall off," Melanie protested.

"Don't get your feathers ruffled. All Vince's riders wear one," Chris explained as she took a vest for herself.

Melanie set her saddle on the back of a desk chair and put on the vest. Outside the door, a huge gray horse stood in the driveway. He was pawing the ground and snorting like a train. A groom was holding tightly to a lead snapped to the bit, but the horse pranced around, paying no attention to him.

Christina nodded toward the open door. "That's Fortune."

"He doesn't look so bad," Melanie said, laughing a little nervously. She zipped the vest and adjusted the side straps. Picking up her saddle, she took a deep breath. She was determined to do her best and not worry about Fortune's Way.

"Hey, are you getting on this horse or what?" the

groom called, his sharp voice startling Melanie. "I've got other horses to tack up, and I'm sick of getting my feet stepped on."

"Oh, right," Melanie said, and hurried out of the office. The groom tossed a pad onto the horse's back, and Melanie set her saddle on top of it. When the groom tightened the girth, Fortune humped his back and squealed.

Melanie grinned. "I can tell he loves me already." She put on her helmet and, just to be safe, lowered her stirrups a notch. If Fortune was a bucker, a deep seat might help her stay in the saddle.

The groom gave her a leg up, then walked them to the gravel path that led to the track. "Good luck," he said as he unsnapped the lead line. "You'll need it."

Gee, thanks, Melanie thought. Taking up the slack on the reins, Melanie let Fortune bounce and hop his way down the path.

As they approached the track Melanie caught sight of Vince Jones. The trainer wore a polo shirt, khakis, and his trademark fedora. A stopwatch hung around his neck, and he was leafing through Turfway's condition book. Keeping one eye on the booklet, he watched Melanie ride up. She gave him her most confident smile.

Just as they reached the gate Fortune abruptly rooted his head, yanking the reins through Melanie's fingers. "Hey!" she hollered, desperately trying to gather them up, but it was too late. Fortune bucked, throwing her onto his neck.

"Good morning, Ms. Graham," Vince called. "Having a little trouble?"

Melanie turned red. With one hand she pushed herself back into the saddle. The other clutched the reins.

"When you *finally* get Fortune on the track," he continued in a voice loud enough for everyone to hear, "just give him a light workout. He isn't racing this weekend."

Several people laughed. Melanie's cheeks burned, and a rush of adrenaline surged through her. Grabbing one rein, Melanie pulled Fortune's head up and around to her knee.

"Two can play this game," she told him as she turned the ornery animal in a circle. When he came out of the circle, she kicked him with her heels, and he leaped through the opening and onto the track.

"Watch out!" a rider hollered. Nervously Melanie steered Fortune away from the horses breezing counterclockwise around the track. His trot was long and springy, throwing her into the air. When she finally found his rhythm, she turned him to the inside rail for a brief gallop.

Fortune broke into a fast, rough canter. Melanie perched forward, trying to use her body and voice to smooth him out. But he hauled on the reins, pulling her off balance. She gritted her teeth, wanting to haul back with all her might, but she knew she'd never win a battle of strength with a thousand-pound horse.

7

She'd have to try something different.

She flexed her fingers on the right hand, then the left, fiddling with the bit, trying to communicate with the hard-mouthed horse. But he clamped the bit between his teeth and ran even harder.

This is useless, Melanie thought with frustration as Fortune thundered past Vince Jones and the other trainers, who were surely laughing at her. The gelding stretched into a gallop and his hooves pounded the dirt track like pistons, jarring Melanie so hard her teeth rattled.

Melanie tried again to slow him, then gave up. Setting her hands high on his neck, she let the reins go slack. Fortune tore around the track, whizzing past the other horses. Finally he slowed on his own, as if bored now that there was no one to fight.

When he slowed to a trot, his sides were heaving. "So much for a light workout," Melanie muttered. Vince would be furious.

She jogged Fortune clockwise along the outside rail to cool him off, then slowed him to a walk and headed to the gate. Melanie grimaced. What was she going to say to Vince?

The trainer had rolled up the condition book and was tapping it against the railing. Melanie gulped hard when she rode up. He definitely looked mad. Fortune bolted through the gate, eager to get back to the barn.

"I tried to keep—" Melanie began as the gelding

jigged past the trainer.

Vince cut her off. "Ride Sneaky Pete next," he barked, immediately turning his attention back to the horses on the track.

"Uh, y-yes, sir," Melanie stammered, not sure she'd heard him right. So he was willing to try her on another horse, even though she'd done so badly with Fortune?

When they reached the barn, Melanie halted, dismounting before the big horse could take off again. Suddenly the gelding swung around and shoved Melanie with his nose, sending her flying into the groom. "Got dumped, huh?" the groom said as he snapped the lead line onto Fortune's bit.

"No, I stayed on," Melanie said. Unbuckling the girth, she slipped off her saddle.

Just then Christina rode up on a light-boned bay filly. Smiling at her cousin, she dismounted. "Congratulations, Mel!" she trumpeted.

"For what? I barely stayed on."

"I heard Vince gave you another horse to ride." Christina pulled off her saddle, and a groom led her horse off. "So you must have done okay." She pointed to a leggy chestnut colt whose legs were being wrapped. "That's Sneaky Pete. He's easy to ride. I'll see you on the track," she added as she rushed off. "I've got to gallop Gratis for his official time."

While Melanie waited for Sneaky Pete to be bri-

9

dled, she propped her saddle against the barn wall, pulled a granola bar from her back pocket, and walked along the row of stalls as she ate. Most of the horses had only mesh stall guards to keep them inside. Thoroughbreds in training spent endless hours in their stalls. At least when the doorways were open, they could stick their heads out and entertain themselves by watching the backside activity.

Melanie stopped in front of the only stall that didn't have a guard. The bottom half was enclosed by a solidly built wooden door. *Newly* built, Melanie realized, noticing the clean wood and shiny screw heads. The upper half was enclosed with a wire mesh door latched in two places.

Melanie looked inside, half expecting to see a fire-breathing dragon. Instead she saw a beautiful coal-black horse with a snippet of white on her nose.

"Image?" Melanie recognized Fredericka Graber's two-year-old filly. Several weeks ago Christina had pointed out the filly to Melanie, telling her that Image was the great-granddaughter of Townsend Holly, the same dam that had foaled Ashleigh's Wonder. Wonder was Star's dam, which meant the two-year-olds had similar bloodlines.

Stepping closer, Melanie peered through the wire mesh. Image was backed into the far corner, but she was looking intently at Melanie. Melanie didn't think the filly was mean. So why was she all locked up?

"Can I help you?" someone asked. Melanie turned. A slender girl about her age, dressed in a T-shirt that said Tall Oaks Farm, had come up behind her.

"I was just looking at Image," Melanie said. She pointed to the two doors. "What's with the jail cell? Did she steal a bag of carrots?" Melanie was joking, but the girl didn't crack a smile.

"We had to build a door because she's an escape artist," the girl said. She had long blond hair pulled back in a barrette and horseshoe-shaped earrings.

"An escape artist?" Melanie repeated.

"Yeah. The first day Image was here, she got out," the blonde continued. "Vince reamed me out for not latching the stall guard properly. Only I knew I had. So after I put her back, I sat over there"—the girl pointed to an empty stall across the way—"and watched. When Image knew no one was around, she crawled under the stall guard."

Melanie's brows rose. The guards were big enough that Image would have had to go down on her knees and belly to creep under, no easy feat for a large animal. "What did she do when she got out?"

"Ran onto the track infield and found a nice patch of grass. She hates being cooped up."

Melanie gazed at the filly with amazement. "Pretty smart."

"Oh, yes," the girl agreed. "But no one else believes me when I tell them how smart she is. Yesterday she

11

used her teeth to lift the wire door off its hinges. I caught her before she figured out how to get the bottom door open."

Melanie looped her fingers through the mesh. Image came over, pressed her nostrils against the wire, and inhaled noisily.

"That's a granola bar you're smelling," Melanie told the inquisitive filly, who gently lipped her fingers. "I'd give you a piece, but I ate it all." She turned to look at the girl, who was still standing behind her. "May I go in and see her?"

Before the girl could say anything, Melanie quickly introduced herself. "I'm Melanie Graham. I just started exercising horses for Mr. Jones. I know Mrs. Graber, Image's owner. My cousin, Christina, rides Gratis for Mr. Jones."

"I'm Elizabeth Wagner, one of Mrs. Graber's grooms. Usually I work at Tall Oaks, Mrs. Graber's farm, but she wanted me to come to the track for the weekend and keep an eye on Image."

"Is something wrong with her?"

"Yeah. She's a big pain in the neck. The track grooms hate to work with her."

"But grooms are used to working with tough horses," Melanie said.

"Image is *worse* than tough," Elizabeth said. Lowering her voice, she said, "She's spoiled rotten. Ever since she was born, she's been Mrs. Graber's pet. When Vince brought Image to the track, Fredericka told him she'd fire anyone who 'abuses' her precious baby. And to Fredericka, abuse means raising your voice."

"No wonder the grooms hate to work with her. Can I see her? If it's okay."

"I guess it's all right." Unlocking all the latches, Elizabeth held the doors open wide enough for Melanie to squeeze through.

Image stood her ground, her ears pricked. Melanie held out her hand. The filly sniffed it, then raised her muzzle to Melanie's face. Delicately she explored Melanie's cheeks and forehead, her whiskers tickling Melanie's skin.

Melanie held her breath, trying not to giggle. When Image dropped her muzzle and nudged her chest as if to say, *I guess you're okay*, Melanie reached up to pat her. She ruffled the filly's forelock, ran her hand down her silky neck, then stepped back to look at her.

She was the most gorgeous horse Melanie had ever seen.

Even in the dim light of the stall, Melanie could see the perfect line of her back, her arched neck, the swell of her muscled hindquarters, her long legs, and her massive shoulders. Image had balance, beauty, and power.

But what drew Melanie most was the gleam of curiosity in the filly's gaze. Image was studying Melanie just as closely as Melanie was studying her. Melanie caught her breath, amazed at the intelligence that radiated from the filly's eyes.

"Maybe all the grooms think you're a pain, but I think you're perfect," Melanie whispered. "No wonder Fredericka spoils you," she added, lightly caressing the filly's neck. "She knows how special you are, and I bet she loves you lots. I think I might have fallen in love with you, too."

2

MELANIE SMILED WISTFULLY. IF ONLY SHE HAD THE CHANCE to ride a horse as gorgeous and powerful as Image!

Too bad it would never happen. Image had the breeding to be a top-notch stakes winner. Vince Jones would hire an experienced jockey to race her, not a bug like Melanie who'd been on a losing streak.

"At least I can ask Vince or Fredericka if I can be your exercise rider," Melanie said. She scratched the filly under her forelock, laughing when Image wiggled her upper lip with pleasure.

Glancing out the stall door, Melanie saw a groom walk past leading Sneaky Pete.

The colt's legs were wrapped, and he was ready to work. She gave Image a departing hug, then slipped through the doorway.

"Thanks for letting me visit Image," Melanie said

to Elizabeth, who was holding a lead line. "Are you getting her ready for her morning works?"

Elizabeth gave her a strange look. "No. I'm just hand-walking her."

"No one's exercising her this morning?"

"No one's riding her at all. She's only at the track to get used to the sights and sounds."

Melanie was confused. "Isn't she a two-year-old?"

"Yeah. But Fredericka wants to wait until Image is more mature and less skittish." Elizabeth opened the doors wider.

"Has she had *any* training?"

"Not much. All Fredericka's done is feed her treats and brush her," Elizabeth said, snapping the lead onto Image's halter ring. "Image is like a thousand-pound pampered poodle."

Melanie swallowed a gulp of laughter.

"I'm not kidding," Elizabeth said as she opened the stall door and led the filly out. "Vince finally *ordered* Fredericka to bring her here and get her training started."

Elizabeth halted Image in the aisle. The filly gazed around, her dark eyes glittering, her nostrils quivering as she took in the sights and scents of the backside.

Melanie hardly heard a word of what Elizabeth was saying. She was too busy staring at Image. The rising sun shone on the filly's black coat, making it gleam like polished ebony. Her dished face and small, pointed ears were delicate, yet her neck, shoulders, and hindquarters looked powerful and built to run. She was awesome.

"Well, I've gotta ride," Melanie said reluctantly, picking up her saddle. The groom was leading Sneaky Pete down the drive, and Melanie hurried to meet them. Glancing over her shoulder, she watched Elizabeth lead Image in the other direction, the filly prancing daintily beside her. Elizabeth's shoulders were stiff, and she held the lead with an iron fist.

Without warning, Image pulled back and reared, her front legs flailing in the air so wildly that Elizabeth lost her balance and fell. The lead line ripped from her grasp, and Image wheeled around and took off at a gallop.

For a second, Melanie was so surprised she just stared at the galloping filly as if she were watching a scene from a movie. But Image was real and was charging straight for her.

"Whoa!" Melanie called. Dropping her saddle, she stretched her arms wide, hoping to slow the black filly down. Image shot her a defiant look, darted around her without missing a beat, and galloped away, her tail streaming.

"Wow," Melanie breathed, admiring the filly's speed and agility. Then she realized that Image was headed for the track.

"Loose horse!" she hollered, sounding the cry that sends chills down every horseperson's spine. As Melanie raced down the path after Image, heads turned, but it was too late. Image bolted through the gap in the railing and onto the track.

Melanie ran after her, with Elizabeth on her heels, but they both stopped when they reached the track. Running blindly into the path of the galloping horses would be foolish and dangerous. As soon as the outriders saw Image, they would signal the other riders to stop their horses until Image was caught.

"Is that Fredericka's crazy filly?" Vince Jones hollered. He stormed over to where Melanie and Elizabeth were standing on the rail. "What's she doing loose? Who let her go?"

Melanie glanced at Elizabeth, whose face had turned pale. "It's my fault, sir," Elizabeth said in a hushed voice. "I was leading her and—"

"It *wasn't* her fault," Melanie cut in. "Image reared for no reason and knocked Elizabeth over. There was no way she could have held on to the lead."

Vince glanced from one girl to the other, his mouth set in an angry line. "We'd better catch her before she crashes into somebody. Stupid filly doesn't have an ounce of sense."

"That's not true," Melanie said. "Image is smarter—"

"Oh, no," Elizabeth gasped, cutting her off.

Melanie swung around to see what was happening. Image was galloping counterclockwise as if she were in a race, holding her head high enough so the lead line wouldn't get tangled in her legs. Two outriders galloped behind her, shouting for people to

18

watch out, and the red light near the three-eighths pole blinked, signaling trouble. About five lengths in front of Image, an unsuspecting Christina and Gratis were breezing on the inside rail.

Christina was hunched over Gratis's neck, following his smooth and steady gallop with her hands. Melanie could tell her cousin hadn't noticed the light or the outriders, and Image was gaining on them with every stride.

"That horse can't be stupid enough to run into them," Vince exclaimed.

But it looked as though that was just what Image was going to do. Not because she was stupid, but because this was a race she was determined to win.

Melanie held her breath as Image pulled alongside Gratis. Only then did Christina tilt her head and see her. With a haughty flick of her tail, Image cut in front of Gratis, and the colt swerved to avoid her, crashing into the inside rail.

The wooden boards made a sickening crack. Melanie clamped her hand over her mouth, stifling a scream as Christina flew off Gratis, somersaulted over the railing, and disappeared from sight on the other side.

"Chris!" Melanie raced across the track. Behind her, someone shouted for the track ambulance.

By the time Melanie reached Gratis, an outrider had ridden up and caught the colt's dangling reins. Gratis stood with his front legs splayed. His head was down, and blood oozed from a gash on his chest.

Putting two hands on the top board, Melanie vaulted over the railing into the infield. Christina was sitting on the grass, holding her head with one hand.

"Chris! Are you all right?" Melanie dropped to her knees beside her cousin.

"I think so," Christina said, her voice quivering.

Melanie put a hand on her cousin's arm. "Don't move. The rescue crew will be here in a second. You may think you're all right, but you could have a concussion or a broken arm or—"

"Mel, calm down. I'm okay." Christina pulled off her helmet and shook out her hair. "What happened? Gratis was breezing along fine, then all of a sudden I was flying over his head."

"You didn't see Image come up beside you?"

"That was Image? What was she doing on the track?"

"She pulled loose from Elizabeth."

"Ms. Reese, are you injured?" a voice barked.

Melanie looked up. Vince Jones was leaning over the railing, breathing hard from the run. Elizabeth was beside him. Tears streaked her cheeks.

"I don't think so," Christina said. "Nothing hurts. I didn't hit the rail. I landed on the grass."

"You could have broken your neck!" Vince said angrily. "Wait until I get my hands on that filly."

Melanie jumped to her feet. "I'll catch her!"

Just then the ambulance drove onto the track and parked on the rail nearby.

"I mean, sir, I think it would be a good idea if you looked at Gratis's wound," Melanie said quickly. "I'll catch Image for you."

Vince glared at her, then swung his gaze to Elizabeth, who seemed to shrink. "Call Lexi and tell her to get a van over here. I want that filly out of my barn and off the track right now. She's been nothing but bad luck since she got here." He turned his attention back to Christina. Two emergency medical technicians had climbed over the railing and were kneeling beside her. "I'm glad you're all right," he said before striding over to Gratis.

Melanie let out her breath. Vince was scary enough, but he was even worse when he was angry.

"Are you going to be okay if I go get Image?" Melanie asked Christina. Her cousin nodded silently. The EMTs had put a blood pressure cuff around her arm and were feeling her all over for breaks.

Melanie cut across the infield. On the other side of the track, an outrider was still trying to catch Image. He was riding a quick little pinto, but Image was faster, and she looked as though she was having fun. Every time the outrider got close enough to snag her lead rope, Image would dart away again. Melanie could almost imagine her laughing.

Vince had said the filly was stupid and skittish, but Melanie knew he was wrong. Prancing around the outrider's pony, Image looked as cunning as a wild horse.

But how do you catch a wild horse? Melanie wondered as she climbed the railing and dropped onto the track.

You can't, was the answer. She'd have to get Image to come to her. Otherwise the outriders and other track workers would corner her, rope her, or wear her down—anything to get her off the track before she hurt someone else, even if it meant badly frightening or hurting Image in the process.

By the time she reached Image, Melanie was puffing. "I'll try to herd her your way," the outrider called.

Melanie halted, caught her breath, and held up her hand. "No. Stop your horse and see if she stops."

"Okay." The outrider halted his horse, who stood patiently. Image halted, too, her head cocked as she stared suspiciously at Melanie. Her neck was slick with sweat, and her nostrils were flared.

Think, Melanie told herself. *Come up with a plan.* Suddenly she remembered what Elizabeth had told her about the first time Image had gotten loose. She'd trotted onto the infield to graze. Melanie spotted a clump of grass peeking under the inside railing.

A bribe might work. After all, Image was tired. Maybe she was also ready to be caught.

"Wow! Look at that grass," Melanie said excitedly, and Image flicked one ear with interest. Moving slowly, Melanie walked over to the clump, pulled up several green hunks, and held it out. "Doesn't this look delicious?"

Ears pricked, Image bobbed her head. She took one step forward.

"Mmm-mmm." Melanie smacked her lips. "I bet it's yummy." Holding the clump to her mouth, she pretended to take a bite. Several people hurried up, ready to help catch the runaway, but the outrider made them stay back.

Image took another step. Melanie stifled the urge to leap forward and grab the lead, because she knew that Image would just wheel and run. She had to be patient. She had to make the filly come to her.

Another step and Image was almost within reach. Melanie smacked her lips again and made chewing sounds. "This is so good. Would you like a bite?" She held it in front of her.

Stretching out her neck, Image sniffed the clump. Melanie drew it back toward her chest, and Image moved closer. When the filly came close enough to pluck a mouthful of grass, Melanie reached around with her free hand and grabbed the rope.

"Gotcha," she whispered.

"Never saw that technique used," the outrider said when he rode up. Melanie handed him the lead line.

"You'd better take her back. I want to see if Gratis and Christina are all right." *And I don't want her getting loose again*, she added to herself, remembering how easily the filly had pulled away from Elizabeth.

"That's Image's groom." Melanie pointed to Elizabeth, who was hanging back in the crowd of onlookers. "You may have to help her get Image to her stall. She's stabled at Vince Jones's barn."

The outrider nodded. Grasping the rope tightly, he snubbed Image's head against his thigh and clucked to his pony. As they rode off, Image pranced alongside, shaking her head defiantly.

Melanie jogged around the track to the ambulance, where Christina was sitting on a cot inside, a bandage on her right wrist. Melanie was glad to see Ashleigh, Christina's mom, next to her daughter, her arm wrapped protectively around Christina's shoulder. Just a few feet away, the track veterinarian was checking Gratis over.

"Are you okay, Chris?" Melanie asked anxiously from outside the ambulance doors.

Christina furrowed her brow. "Yeah. My wrist hurts, but the EMT said it was just sprained. I must have broken my fall with my hand."

"Thank goodness she didn't break the bone," Ashleigh said, her face pale with worry. Ashleigh had grown up training and racing horses, so she'd had her share of accidents. But Melanie knew her aunt was always terrified that Christina or Melanie would get hurt.

"Do you think you can still ride in the race tomorrow?" Melanie asked her cousin.

"Absolutely not," Ashleigh said firmly. "We'll get another jockey for Star."

"*No!*" Christina cried, and Melanie's heart fell

when she saw the shock and disappointment on her cousin's face.

"You're not racing, Christina," Ashleigh repeated. "It may be only a sprain, but we can't take any chances. You're very lucky. Look at Gratis." She nodded toward the colt. "He's going to need stitches, and Vince is going to have to pull him from Sunday's race. And if that cut's deep enough and the muscle doesn't heal, Gratis may never race again."

"Don't say that!" Melanie glanced uneasily at Vince. He and the vet were deep in conversation, their expressions grim. The vet was holding a wad of thick gauze against Gratis's chest, but blood continued to seep through the bandage.

Melanie groaned in dismay. Christina and Aunt Ashleigh hadn't said anything about Image, but they didn't need to. The whole disaster was Image's fault.

3

"I'm sorry you can't ride tomorrow, Chris," Melanie apologized to her cousin, as if somehow she were to blame and not Image.

"What do you mean, 'can't ride'?" Christina said, suddenly looking very determined. "Mom, there's no way you're putting another jockey on Star tomorrow. I've got to ride him." Holding up her bandaged arm, she flexed her wrist. "I'll be fine."

Ashleigh shook her head. "I don't know, Chris. If you can't hold the reins—"

"She can do it." Melanie came to her cousin's defense. "Christina's tough, and Star's not a puller." She knew how important the next day's race was to her cousin.

Ashleigh rolled her eyes. "You two don't know when to quit, do you?"

26

"Something we learned from you," Melanie said, grinning at her aunt.

With a sigh, Ashleigh crossed her arms over her chest and gazed steadily at her daughter, weighing the options. "All right. But if your wrist swells or gets worse—"

Before Ashleigh could finish, Christina threw her arms around her mother and hugged her. "Thank you!"

Christina hopped from the ambulance, and Ashleigh climbed out after her. A groom was leading Gratis slowly toward the gate, with Vince and the veterinarian right behind them.

"Is Vince furious at Image?" Melanie asked Christina in a low voice.

"Oh, yes." Christina nodded as the three walked across the track. "He's getting Lexi to come and take her back to Fredericka's farm right away."

"I guess I can't blame him. Who's Lexi?" Melanie asked curiously.

"Alexis Huffman. She's Fredericka's farm manager," Ashleigh explained. "I don't blame Vince, either. It looks as though Image needs to learn some manners before she comes back to the track."

"But Image's groom says no one wants to work with her because she's too spoiled and difficult." She told Christina and Ashleigh about her conversation with Elizabeth. "I wonder what Fredericka will do with her," she added.

Ashleigh gave Melanie a curious look. "Why are you so interested in Image?"

"I don't know, I just am," Melanie answered with a shrug. She led the way through the gate, dodging the horses and riders who were coming back onto the track now that it had been cleared. She wasn't sure why, but her heart raced as they approached Vince's barn. She couldn't wait to find out what was going to happen to Image.

Fredericka had arrived and was standing in the middle of the wide aisle between the shed rows, talking to Vince, who gestured angrily toward Image's stall. As always, Fredericka was dressed as if she were at a formal garden party. She wore an elegant green dress, tan mules, and a straw hat decorated with silk flowers.

As Vince railed on and on, Fredericka nodded earnestly. Melanie didn't know Fredericka well but had always been impressed by her charm and graciousness.

"What do you think Vince is saying?" Melanie whispered to Christina.

"That her idiot of a filly almost killed me and her prize colt," Christina guessed.

Melanie bristled. "Image is not an idiot. In fact, she's really smart."

"Maybe too smart," Ashleigh commented. "Come on, Chris. I want to see how Gratis is doing."

Ashleigh and Christina headed for the colt's stall at

the end of the shed row. Melanie hung back and quietly edged toward Image's stall.

Once again Image was locked in behind the metal gate. Elizabeth sat on a folding chair next to the door, sipping a soda. She was hunched over, her elbows on her knees. Tears had left tracks on her dirt-smudged cheeks.

"Are you okay?" Melanie asked.

"Oh, sure," Elizabeth said, her tone sarcastic. "Vince just banished me and Image from the track." She took a sip of her drink, then added, "Not that I mind, I guess. I'd much rather be back at Tall Oaks working with the babies." She sighed. "Still, I feel like such a screw-up. Thanks for sticking up for me, though."

"It wasn't your fault." Melanie peered into the stall. "Is Image all right?" The sweat had dried on the filly's neck, and she was eating her breakfast hay as if the morning romp had never happened.

"I guess. I rubbed her down with a towel, but I didn't dare hose her off. If she got loose again, Vince would go ballistic."

Melanie gestured toward the stall door. "Mind if I go in and check her legs? She ran pretty hard out there."

"Be my guest."

"Hey, girl," Melanie crooned when she went inside. Laying her palm on the filly's chest, she checked to see if she was cool. Then she ran a hand down each front leg. Image glanced once at her, then continued to eat her hay. "Is Lexi coming to take her away?" Melanie called out to Elizabeth.

"Yeah. She'll be here in about half an hour with the van."

"Where's she taking her?"

"Back to Tall Oaks, Fredericka's farm."

Which means I won't see you again. Melanie stroked Image's neck, her heart growing heavy. As she finished checking the filly's hind legs, she wondered what would happen to Image when she went back to Tall Oaks. Would she be dumped in some big pasture and forgotten? Would someone try to work with her?

"Uh-oh," Elizabeth said in a low voice. "Here comes Vince. Do you mind watching Image while I disappear? I really can't take him yelling at me again."

"Sure, go ahead." Melanie straightened. Through the mesh door she could see Vince and Fredericka walking toward the stall. Fredericka was frowning worriedly. Vince had a determined expression on his face.

"She's got impeccable breeding," Vince was saying. "But she's brainless, and a disaster on the track. Breed her next spring to a stallion that's got some brains and manners, and maybe her foals will be racing material."

"Well, that's good advice, Vince," Fredericka replied in her soft voice. "And you know I trust your advice, but don't you think we're giving up too soon?"

"Too soon?" Stopping in his tracks, Vince turned to face Fredericka, his scowl deepening. "We were lucky Christina and Gratis weren't killed! I've already told you—Image is just too skittish and half-witted to race. Do you need another disaster before you decide to give up and let her be a broodmare?"

"No, no." Fredericka glanced toward Image's stall, an anguished look in her eyes. "You're right."

No, he's not right. Don't listen to him, Fredericka, Melanie wanted to shout. She remembered how easily Image had caught up to and passed Gratis. The filly had racing in her blood. She deserved a chance.

She is a little nuts, though, Melanie reminded herself. Image definitely needed someone to teach her some manners. *Someone who is patient and determined and loves Image enough to want her to succeed,* she decided. *Someone like me.*

When Melanie glanced out the door again, Vince had gone, and Fredericka stood in front of the stall, looking concerned.

Melanie opened the top door halfway and peered out. "Hello, Mrs. Graber. I'm Melanie Graham, Christina Reese's cousin. I met you about a week ago."

Despite her obvious worry, Fredericka smiled warmly. "Yes, I remember. You were Star's jockey when he beat Gratis." Her smile faded when she looked into the stall. "Thank you for catching Image for me. My beautiful princess behaved very badly today, didn't she?"

31

At the sound of her owner's voice, Image gave a throaty whinny. Shoving the top door with her nose, she stuck her head out. Hastily Melanie latched the bottom door. The last thing they needed was for Image to escape again.

"No, I don't have an apple for you today, my love," Fredericka said. "But when you get back to Tall Oaks, I'll have lots of treats for you."

"I know it's none of my business, Mrs. Graber, but I don't agree with Mr. Jones," Melanie said.

"Don't agree with what, dear?"

"I don't think Image is half-witted at all. I think she's smart, maybe too smart for her own good. And skittish? No way. She knew exactly what she was doing when she pulled away from Elizabeth and ran onto the track." As she talked, Melanie's voice rose excitedly. Fredericka appeared to be hanging on her every word. "And wow, is she fast!" Melanie went on. "You should have seen her galloping around the track. She was trying to beat Gratis, and she did it!"

"Oh, Melanie, I'm so glad you told me all this," Fredericka said, beaming happily. "I've always felt that Image was special, and if only someone could train her, she could be a champion runner. But I'm afraid what Vince said is true," she added, her excitement dimming. "No one can train her, and it's all my fault."

"Why is it your fault?" Melanie asked.

Sighing, Fredericka held her delicate, ringed fingers out to the black filly. Image snuffled her hand curiously, then returned to her hay.

"Image was born the same day my beloved husband, Charles, died," Fredericka explained. "His death was devastating. But Image was absolutely the most beautiful foal I had ever seen, and she comforted me. I spent hours with her, something I'd never done with any of my other horses. I must admit I spoiled her rotten, though I knew it might wind up doing more damage than good. And now you see the results." Fredericka shook her head. "No one will ever be able to train Image, because she doesn't know she's a horse. She thinks she's human and entitled to all the same rights and privileges."

"Then let me try!" Melanie interrupted, unable to hold her tongue any longer.

Fredericka's brows rose. "Try what?"

"Training her. Not here, but at your farm. I bet Image loves to run—she was bred to—and if she's as smart as we think she is, then she deserves a chance."

"Well." Fredericka took a deep breath. "You do seem determined. But what makes you think *you* can train her if Vince can't?"

Melanie bit her lip, hoping she'd say the right things to convince Fredericka to let her try. She took a deep breath and began. "Because just like you do, I think Image is special. She's clever and quick, but kind of stubborn and headstrong. She's a free spirit. I know this might sound silly . . ." Melanie hesitated, her cheeks reddening as she continued in a hoarse whisper. "But I think Image is a lot like me."

A slow smile spread across Fredericka's face. "Well, then, Melanie Graham, you deserve a chance to work with my Image. Come to Tall Oaks on Monday after the racing weekend. I'll show you the facilities and introduce you to everyone. Then we'll see what happens."

"Thank you!" Melanie exclaimed. Grabbing Fredericka's hand, she gave it a squeeze. Then she turned and clasped Image around the neck.

"Did you hear that, Image?" Melanie exclaimed in a rush of excitement—the kind of excitement she hadn't felt in a long, long time.

4

THE THOROUGHBREDS FLEW DOWN TURFWAY'S TRACK IN A tight pack. Melanie glanced right, then left, trying to find a hole. They were at the three-quarter-mile pole, and it was time to make a move.

It was Saturday, and Melanie was riding Mischief Maker, one of Whitebrook's horses, in the Maple Leaf Allowance Race. Mischief had plenty of go, but the field of horses was racing so tightly, there was nowhere for her *to* go.

Over the roar of the crowd Melanie heard the announcer calling the horses' names and positions. The wind and the thud of hooves filled her ears. Dirt clumps stung her cheeks and speckled the lenses of her goggles. Exhilaration caused goose bumps to rise on her arms.

Just wait till I'm riding Image in a race, Melanie

thought excitedly. For a second she imagined that the horse moving beneath her was Image. They were thundering to the finish line, lengths ahead, the track stretched out before them.

"Outta my way!" a jockey hollered, startling Melanie from her reverie. George Valdez, one of the older, tougher jockeys, glared at her from aboard his mount, Sweet Majesty. Mischief Maker had strayed so far to the right that George was only inches away, close enough for Melanie to reach out and tap his shoulder.

"Sorry!" Melanie yelled. Flexing the fingers of her left hand, she signaled Mischief to move toward the inside rail, which was where she wanted to be. But four other horses were already there, battling for position.

Dead ahead of her, Vicky Frontiere, another seasoned jockey, was riding Baby Cakes. Beside Melanie against the rail, Tommy Turner jockeyed Pretty Penny. With George's mount still galloping on the right, Melanie and Mischief were boxed in.

Melanie gritted her teeth, trying to find a hole so she could move up. Two months earlier she would have charged recklessly through any opening. But after her accident on Fast Gun . . .

Don't think about the accident, Melanie told herself. *Just go for it.*

Baby Cakes surged ahead, George's horse swung wide, and Melanie spotted her chance. Hunkering down on Mischief Maker's neck, she steered the filly through the narrow gap between the two horses.

Mischief's stride lengthened, and she pulled along-side Baby Cakes just as they passed under the wire.

"It's Baby Cakes by a nose!" the announcer hollered.

Melanie's heart fell. Second place—*again*.

Standing in her stirrups, she slowed Mischief to a canter. George steered Sweet Majesty beside them. "Better quit daydreaming out there," he hollered, his tone threatening. "'Cause if you run into me, you're dead meat."

"Sorry, my goggles got dirty," Melanie fibbed. She didn't dare tell him she'd lost her concentration. There was no place for daydreaming in the middle of a race.

But the truth was that Melanie couldn't stop herself from thinking about Image. She couldn't wait until Monday. Image was so smart and fast . . . and beautiful.

When she dismounted and handed the reins to Mike Reese, Christina's father, Melanie was grinning happily, despite her second-place finish.

"That was a good race!" Mike said. "Congratulations."

"Thanks, Uncle Mike." Melanie pulled the reins over Mischief's head, then gave the filly's glistening neck a pat. "I'm sorry we sort of got boxed in at the end."

"Maybe we'll try her at a mile and a quarter next time," Mike said, adjusting the brim of his Whitebrook Farm baseball cap.

Melanie unbuckled Mischief's girth and slid off her saddle.

"Good luck on your next ride," Mike said before leading Mischief away.

"Thanks," Melanie called. She had been living at Whitebrook for four years and had come to love Ashleigh and Mike like a second set of parents.

As Melanie walked back to the jockey's room she thought wistfully about her own father, who lived in New York. Will Graham hadn't grown up around horses and didn't really understand Melanie's passion. But when he saw Image, Melanie knew, he'd be as excited and impressed as she was. How could he not be?

She pulled open the door to the jockey room, but someone bumped her aside.

"Oh, excuse me," a familiar voice said sarcastically, and George pushed ahead of her, chuckling as he went through the door.

Melanie hurried after him. "What was that for?" she demanded angrily.

"That was for the bump on the track," George said matter-of-factly. He snatched up his duffel bag and strode quickly into the men's locker room.

"I did not bump you!" Melanie shouted after him. Turning, she noticed that the half-dozen jockeys in the waiting area were watching her. "I didn't," she said again before plopping down on the worn sofa in front of the TV, where her race was being replayed.

When the galloping horses passed the three-quarter pole, Melanie saw Mischief Maker swerve into Sweet Majesty's path. Melanie grimaced. She hadn't bumped George, but she was definitely guilty of losing her focus.

Winning the Breeder's Futurity on Star had built up her confidence a little bit, but Melanie knew it wasn't enough. If she didn't start doing a better job, she was going to end up riding claimers for the rest of the year, and maybe the rest of her career.

Christina came out of the women's locker area and sat on the arm of the sofa. She was riding Star for Whitebrook, so she wore a blue-and-white helmet cover and racing silks.

Melanie cocked her head toward her. "Don't say it."

"Say what?" Christina looked puzzled.

"What a lousy job I did in the race."

"What do you mean? You got second—what's wrong with that? I was just going to tell you about Favorite Game, Phil Oberman's colt. Aren't you riding him in the last race?"

"Oh. Yeah."

"Well, he's a powerful runner, but he zigzags all over the track, so you're going to have to give him a really strong ride."

Melanie sat up in a huff. "Meaning my last race *wasn't* strong?"

"No, I didn't mean that at all." Christina frowned down at her. "Why are you so touchy?"

"I don't know. Sorry I barked at you," she apologized. "And thanks for the tip on Favorite Game. I'm riding Go for Broke in the sixth race. Do you know anything about him?"

"No, but Fred Anderson has ridden him."

Fred was another bug. "Thanks. I'll ask him," Melanie said, looking around. Fred was sitting at the other end of the room.

"Did you decide if you're going to go with me and Parker to the concert tomorrow night?" Christina asked.

On Sunday night the race weekend would conclude with a concert and fireworks on the infield. Christina and Parker Townsend, Christina's boyfriend, were going and had asked Melanie to come along. Melanie wanted to go to the concert. Her favorite band, U Got It, was playing, but since she'd stopped dating Kevin McLean, she felt like a third wheel whenever she went anywhere with Christina and Parker.

"No," she finally replied. "I think I'll go back to Whitebrook in the horse van with Maureen and Dani."

"But you love U Got It," Christina insisted. She cocked her head, catching Melanie's gaze. "Does this have something to do with Kevin?" she asked gently.

"No," Melanie protested. But she could tell that her cousin didn't believe her.

Melanie didn't want to admit to anyone how much she missed being with Kevin. Not that they'd seen much of each other over the summer, which was the reason they'd broken up. Melanie was too busy with racing, and Kevin was too busy working at Whitebrook and playing in a summer soccer league. There had been no time to hang out, and with senior year of school coming, things would be even harder.

"Well, I gotta go." Christina stood up, her saddle in her arms. "Let me know if you change your mind."

"How's your wrist?"

Holding up her arm, Christina rotated her hand. "I've got an Ace bandage on it. I guess I'll be okay."

"You don't sound too sure."

"I *am* a little nervous," Christina admitted. "After your win on Star in the Futurity, the newspaper reporters and TV newscasters are all debating whether I'll blow it. I hope I do as well as you did."

"You'll do better," Melanie said, grinning. "I'll be rooting for you."

When Christina left, Melanie headed across the room to sit by Fred. He was eighteen and had been a lightweight high-school wrestler. He wasn't much taller than Melanie, but he had broad shoulders and a thick neck and chest. He was a good jockey, but he hadn't grown up around horses and was learning the hard way, riding claimers for small-time trainers. Melanie admired how gutsy Fred was. Even though he was dumped weekly, he hadn't given up.

"Hey, Fred. I heard you rode Go for Broke before."

"Go for Broke," Fred repeated, scrunching up his tanned face. He had brown hair streaked blond by the sun and light blue eyes.

"June Fortig's colt?" Melanie prompted.

"Right!" Fred nodded, suddenly remembering. "Almost killed me in the starting gate."

Melanie groaned.

Fred laughed. "Gotcha. Actually he was a nice ride. The first horse I didn't fall off until *after* we finished the race," he added jokingly.

Melanie laughed. "You're doing better," she joked. "Any tips?"

"Yeah . . . um . . ." Fred blushed, and Melanie wondered what was so embarrassing. "Here's a great tip. This guy I know would love to go with you to tomorrow night's concert."

Melanie frowned. "What—? Oh!" She felt her face grow hot. Fred was asking her out!

"Uh, and the guy's me," Fred added, ducking his head. Melanie gulped. Fred was a great guy, but she'd never thought about going out with him. Still, how could she say no? Besides, she wanted to go to the concert.

"Yeah, that sounds like fun. Can we double with Christina and her boyfriend?"

Fred's face broke into a huge grin. "Sure."

They worked out the details, then Melanie turned her attention to the TV, where Christina and Star were already in the gate for the Turfway Two-Year-Old Classic. Christina had drawn the number-ten gate, a lousy spot in the large field. But Star broke well. He was a powerful distance runner, and Christina let him take his time on the outside, wearing the other horses down. Then she moved Star close to the rail to run beside the flagging leader, a dappled gray called Two of Spades. The duo ran neck and neck for a brief time.

Then Melanie saw Christina's mouth move as if she was calling to Star, and suddenly the colt burst ahead, beating Two of Spades by a couple of lengths.

"You go, girl!" Melanie cheered, jumping to her feet. *They make it look so easy,* she thought. And Melanie knew why. Christina knew how to communicate with Star. In fact, Melanie swore they could talk to each other.

Melanie bet she knew what Christina had been saying to Star when they neared the finish line: *Win this for me.* And Star had responded because the two loved and trusted each other.

"Great race," Fred said.

Melanie sat down, her thoughts turning to Image. Already she could feel a connection between them. Not love or trust, not yet. But there was definitely *something;* Melanie just couldn't put it into words. If she could learn to communicate with Image the way Christina communicated with Star, Image could run just as well as Star; or even better.

Melanie danced to the music, sweat rolling down her forehead. Beside her, Parker and Christina clapped and whistled as U Got It played the last chorus of their most popular song, "Jam with Me."

Strumming his guitar, Mikey Krash, the lead singer for U Got It, belted out the last line. The drummer beat his drums and cymbals in a frenzy, and the backup singers gyrated and wailed.

"You gotta jam with me!" Melanie sang along, her words drowned by the roar of the crowd. It was Sunday night, and Turfway's infield was packed with swaying bodies. On the raised stage, pink and blue lights illuminated the band.

Fred sang along with Melanie, his voice cracking. He was dressed in khaki shorts and a baggy T-shirt, his hair gelled into spikes. When the band blasted out their last line, the crowd clamored for more, but the band waved and trotted off the stage.

"Wow!" Parker said. He was holding Christina's hand. Both their faces glistened with perspiration. It was a warm night, and the crush of dancing people had made it feel even hotter.

"They were the coolest!" Melanie exclaimed. "I mean the *hottest*," she added with a laugh. "I'm so glad I came." She smiled at Fred. Neither Go for Broke nor Favorite Game had placed in their races, and the concert had brightened her spirits.

"Talking about hot, I need a soda or something," Christina said as the foursome slowly moved across the infield, propelled by the pack of departing bodies.

"How about a swim?" Parker asked.

"That sounds even better!" Christina exclaimed. "Where?"

Parker's eyes twinkled. "We could join my parents at an exclusive party at Monty Freedman's."

Fred's eyes widened. "*The* Monty Freedman? One of the track owners?"

"Right."

Christina looked doubtful. "I don't know, Parker. Isn't that crashing?"

"No way. Good old Monty said I should stop by, and my parents will be there. Besides, the Freedmans have a pool that looks like it belongs in paradise, and I doubt the old folks are going to dive in. It might ruin their toupees," he added with a chuckle.

"A swim sounds great to me," Melanie said, fanning herself with her hand. "And they've gotta have something cool to drink."

"All right," Christina relented. "We'll have to stop at the house and get bathing suits."

Parker gave her a funny look. "Bathing suits? You've got to be kidding."

"You mean . . ." Christina looked so flustered, Melanie started to giggle. "He means we can just wear our shorts, silly. I'm in. How about you, Fred?"

Fred looked hesitant. Melanie guessed that he was a little stunned by the thought of diving into Monty Freedman's pool in his sweaty clothes. But Parker did this sort of thing all the time.

"Don't worry. As long as we're with Parker, we'll be fine."

"Sure." Fred shrugged, smiling bashfully. "Why not?"

By the time they reached the parking lot, the crowd had thinned out.

"Can we all fit in your truck, Parker?" Melanie

45

asked. She didn't really want to ride alone with Fred. That would feel too much like a real date.

"Hey, guys!" someone shouted. "Wait up!"

Melanie turned and saw Kevin pushing his way through the people coming out of the infield. Melanie's heart gave a little jump, but then she saw that he was with Lindsay Devereaux, the girl he'd taken to Henry Clay High School's fall dance. Lindsay was tall, blond, and very pretty. It was hard not to feel jealous of her.

Melanie resisted the urge to grab Fred's hand. Fred was a friend, and Melanie wasn't going to use him to make Kevin jealous.

"Wasn't the band awesome?" Lindsay asked. She was a senior at Henry Clay, so she knew everybody, including Parker, who'd graduated the year before.

After they finished talking about the concert, Melanie introduced Fred. Melanie noticed that Kevin gave Fred the once-over before nodding hello.

"Why don't you guys come swimming with us?" Parker asked, and told Kevin and Lindsay about their plans.

Melanie groaned inwardly. It was nice to see Kevin again, but she didn't particularly want to be with him *and* his date.

"Yeah, come with us, you guys. It'll be fun!" Christina chimed in.

When Kevin and Lindsay enthusiastically agreed, Melanie nearly cringed. After getting directions, the group broke up. Melanie followed Fred to his car, a beat-up Datsun. He opened the passenger-side door, apologizing for the mess as he scooped up boots, soda cans, and clothes.

"Looks like you live in here," Melanie teased.

Fred flushed red. "Well, actually sometimes I do when I'm on the road and don't have enough money for a motel."

"Oh," Melanie said, feeling stupid. Out of the corner of her eye, she watched Kevin escort Lindsay to his dad's car. Kevin had gotten his driver's license a week earlier, but it was the first time Melanie had seen him driving without Ian or Beth McLean, his parents. She was surprised by how much it hurt to see him driving with another girl.

Oh, get over it, Melanie told herself, forcing herself to look away from Kevin and Lindsay. The two were laughing and looked so happy together. Melanie had to face the facts, no matter how much it hurt: She and Kevin were no longer a couple.

"I keep thinking if I hang in there long enough, I'll get to ride one great horse," Fred said, starting up the Datsun.

"I know what you mean," Melanie replied, instantly thinking of Image. She smiled, forgetting about Kevin and Lindsay and Saturday's not-so-hot races. The next morning she was going to Tall Oaks to work with Image. That was all that mattered.

5

"So ARE ALL THE RACING BIGWIGS GOING TO BE AT THIS party?" Fred asked, breaking into Melanie's thoughts as they drove out of the parking lot. The Datsun didn't have air-conditioning, so Melanie rolled down the window.

"Probably," Melanie guessed, the humid air blasting her face. "If Brad and Lavinia Townsend are there, it's got to be pretty fancy. I just hope Parker and his parents avoid each other. Brad and Lavinia can be so snotty."

Fred's mouth dropped. "Brad Townsend is Parker's dad?"

Melanie nodded. "Yeah, poor guy."

"What do you mean, poor guy?" Fred countered. "I'd give my soul to live somewhere like Townsend Acres. I was there once when I was a groom, picking up a colt." He whistled. "It was amazing."

Melanie glanced around at Fred's beat-up Datsun, filled with all his possessions. Many of the bugs were like Fred, scraping by until they were good enough to ride in the more lucrative races. Melanie sometimes forgot how lucky she was to live at Whitebrook. Her aunt and uncle's farm might not be as fancy as Townsend Acres, but it was still wonderful. There was an exercise track, big turnouts, and nice, knowledgeable staff; the horses all had top bloodlines; and the place ran like clockwork under Mike and Ashleigh. It was the perfect place to learn to be a jockey.

When they reached the Freedmans', Fred followed Parker's pickup truck up the long, tree-lined drive. Melanie's eyes widened when she saw the fancy cars parked along the front lawn—Porsches, Jaguars, BMWs, and several limousines, their chauffeurs standing beside them. Beyond the cars, the Freedmans' mansion rose into the starlit sky like a movie set from *Gone with the Wind.*

Parker zoomed into an empty spot next to a white limo. Fred pulled beside him and killed the engine. For a second he and Melanie sat in the car, listening to the sounds of laughter and music.

"My Datsun looks a little conspicuous next to all these limos," Fred said finally, sounding nervous. Melanie was feeling a little nervous, too. After all, they were dressed in shorts and T-shirts and hadn't *really* been invited.

Striding over, Parker rapped on the driver's window. "Come on, Fred. Don't let the luxury cars scare you off. This will be a good opportunity for you to rub elbows with some trainers. Maybe you can get a few rides next weekend on some good horses."

Fred glanced at Melanie, and she shrugged. "He's right. The worst the Freedmans can do is kick us out."

They climbed out of the car, joining the others. Melanie though Kevin looked a little hesitant as well, but Lindsay was chattering on and on about the lifestyles of the rich and famous.

As they walked up the drive Christina stopped and pointed to a blue sedan. "There's Mom and Dad's car. They said they were going to a party, but I didn't know they were coming *here*."

"That's a relief," Kevin said. "I was getting a little worried that the party patrol might not let us in." He nodded toward two men dressed in suits who were hanging around the end of the driveway.

Lindsay giggled. "Do you think they'll frisk us?"

"Nah. Just let me handle it." Taking Christina's hand, Parker led the way. When the two men discreetly stopped them, Parker told them who he was. "Check the guest list," he said, his voice oozing confidence.

Melanie had to bite her bottom lip to keep from laughing. Parker worked hard to be the opposite of his parents, but obviously he could act like a Townsend when it suited him.

The two guards glanced at each other, then looked back at the kids. "Sorry, it's not casual attire," the heavyset one said. "I'm afraid we can't let you in."

"Parker!" someone called heartily, and Brad strode up, a cocktail glass in his hand. Dressed in white pants with a perfect crease, his signature navy blazer with gold buttons, a crisp white shirt, and a blue cravat, Brad looked as though he were about to sail off on a yacht. "Glad to see you could make it, son." He put his arm around Parker as if they were the closest father and son in the world. "Monty was asking about you."

Christina looked at Melanie and rolled her eyes. In front of an audience, Brad Townsend could deftly play any part he chose.

Without acknowledging the security guards, Brad proceeded to lead his son toward the mansion. Turning, Parker beckoned to the others. "Come on, guys. We're in."

They headed down a brick walk to the back of the mansion, where fifty people in dress shirts and ties or cocktail dresses talked, danced, and ate, and a five-piece ensemble played big-band tunes. The brick terrace swept around a huge pool. A small waterfall, surrounded by flowering shrubs, flowed into the pool, which shimmered with rainbow-colored lights.

Brad led Parker, Christina, Kevin, and Lindsay over to a group of people and began to introduce them. Stopping at the edge of the terrace, Fred looked around, his mouth open in awe. "Wow," he whispered.

Wow is right, Melanie thought. The Freedmans sure knew how to throw a party.

"Come on, let's see if we can find my aunt and uncle." Feeling as conspicuous as Fred's Datsun, Melanie wound her way through the groups of bejeweled society women, looking for Ashleigh and Mike. She spotted them taking a breather in one corner of the dance floor.

Mike had loosened his tie and unbuttoned the top button of his light blue shirt. Ashleigh wore a pale green silk sheath. Her brown hair was pulled up in a fancy do, but she'd kicked off her shoes and was going barefoot.

"I almost didn't recognize you guys," Melanie said when she hurried up to them.

"Mel! What are you doing here?" Ashleigh asked.

"Parker convinced us we just *had* to make an appearance at the Freedmans' or we'd be erased from the social register," Melanie replied in her best snooty accent.

Mike laughed. "That must be why we're here. That and the food. You ought to grab something to eat," he said to Fred, who was gazing longingly at a table heaped with goodies.

"I think I will," Fred said, and made a beeline for the stack of white plates at the end of the buffet table.

"Chris and Parker are with Brad and Lavinia," Melanie said, pointing them out. "Brad's introducing them to everyone, pretending that he and Parker are best buddies."

"They *are* father and son," Mike said. "And I think that deep down Brad is proud of Parker. Not many kids have the talent and drive to be a contender for the Olympics."

"I guess," Melanie said, suddenly feeling very hungry herself. "I think I'll get something to eat, too. Have fun dancing," she added when the music started up again.

She sauntered over to the table, which was covered with silver platters. There were sliced turkey, fresh shrimp, pork dumplings, stuffed mushrooms, crab cakes, bowls of caviar, crusty French bread and Brie, Caesar salad, chocolate cake, and strawberries, and in the middle of the table was a huge ice sculpture of a horse.

Melanie was filling her plate when she felt an arm steal around her shoulder. Looking up, she saw Brad beaming down at her. She froze, wondering what he wanted.

"I hear you're going to work with Fredericka Graber's filly," he said in his smooth, country-gentleman voice.

"Uh, yeah," Melanie said, not sure why he was interested. And how did he know about it, anyway?

"And just what do you hope to accomplish?" Brad asked, cocking one eyebrow.

Melanie clutched her plate tightly. She knew Brad wasn't asking just to make conversation. He had a reason—but what was it?

"I think with the right training, she'll do well on the track," Melanie said cautiously.

Throwing back his head, Brad laughed loudly. "That's the funniest thing I've ever heard. Image is *never* going to race," he said, squeezing Melanie's shoulder to emphasize the word *never*.

"What makes you so sure?" Melanie countered. "You of all people know her breeding. She's out of Townsend Mistress and a great-granddaughter to Townsend Holly, Wonder's dam. Remember Wonder, the horse you never thought would win anything, much less the Kentucky Derby? And what about Star? He hasn't done too badly for himself."

Brad shrugged as if unconcerned, but Melanie knew by the red hue of his neck that she'd made him mad. "It takes more than good bloodlines to be a winner," he said. "From what I've seen, the horse is too crazy to run. Fredericka should take Vince's advice and turn her into a broodmare—or sell her."

"Well, I think she deserves a chance," Melanie insisted.

Brad frowned. "And what makes you think you're the one to train her?"

It was that same question Fredericka had asked, but Melanie couldn't give the same answer to Brad that she'd given Fredericka: *Because Image and I are just alike.* Brad would only laugh at her. She bit her lip. After all, she'd never trained a horse in her life. How *was* she qualified to train Image?

54

When Melanie didn't say anything, Brad gave her a smug look. "That's what I thought. Well, good luck 'training' her," he said, sauntering away to greet another party goer.

"Don't let him get to you," someone said. Melanie glanced over her shoulder. Kevin stood behind her, a plate in his hand.

"You heard all that?" she asked.

"Some. I wasn't trying to eavesdrop," he explained quickly. "I was getting shrimp and heard you."

"I don't know why he brought it up," Melanie said. "Image isn't any of his business."

"I know why he brought it up. He's still mad about selling Image's dam to Fredericka."

Melanie pricked up her ears. "Really?"

Walking next to the table, Kevin filled his plate while he talked. "You know Brad hates imperfection. So when Townsend Mistress lost her first foal, he figured she was a loser. He sold her to Charles Graber for big bucks. I remember him boasting to my dad about the great deal he'd made. Well, the Grabers got the last laugh. Townsend Mistress went on to have four foals. Two are big-time stakes winners. After the second foal, Brad tried to buy her back, but Charles wouldn't sell her."

"How do you know all this?"

He laughed. "My dad, of course. He knows everything that goes on at every farm in Lexington. And he's doubly interested if it concerns the Townsends.

It's like a soap opera." Kevin gave Melanie a curious look. "Why are *you* so interested in Image?"

As they walked over and sat at a table, Melanie told him about Image. "I think she has great potential!" she finished, her eyes shining. "Fredericka does, too. I'm so glad she's given me a chance to work with her. I start tomorrow morning. I can't wait. Except . . ." Her voice trailed off.

"Except what?" Kevin prompted.

"I'm *not* a trainer, and Image *is* going to be a handful," Melanie admitted with a frown. "Hey!" Reaching across the table, she put her hand on Kevin's arm. "Do you think you could help? You've got so much experience. Together I bet we could do it. Image has really rotten manners, and I remember how well you handled—"

"Whoa." Kevin put up his other hand to stop her. "Melanie, I'd love to help, but once school starts on Tuesday, I've got soccer practice every afternoon, and in the mornings I work at Whitebrook. In between I've got to fit in homework. I have to keep my grades up if I'm going to get a soccer scholarship for college next year."

Melanie's hand slid off his arm. "Oh, right. I know all that," she said, trying not to look as dejected as she felt.

"Kevin!" Lindsay ran over, breathless with excitement. "Come on! Everybody's going swimming! Christina already pushed Parker in."

Melanie looked over at the pool. Parker was climbing out, dripping wet, with a mock expression of anger

56

directed at Christina. Laughing hysterically, Christina darted away from him.

"Let's go, Kevi!" Grabbing Kevin's hand, Lindsay tugged him to his feet.

Kevi? Melanie scrunched up her face.

"Melanie? Are you coming?" Kevin asked.

"In a minute. I need to eat something first." Picking up her fork, Melanie stabbed a shrimp.

When Lindsay led Kevin away, Melanie blew out her breath. She knew Kevin was too busy to help. Why had she even asked? Holding up the fork, she bit the shrimp in half. Loud shrieks and splashes told her someone else had jumped—or been thrown—into the pool.

Glancing around, Melanie saw Fred deep in conversation with Jimmy J, a trainer who'd been around forever. Then she spotted Brad, who was regaling a group with racing stories.

Melanie knew why she'd asked Kevin—because Brad had reminded her that she *wasn't* a trainer. She had worked with lots of horses before, but none like Image, and never all on her own.

But you and Image have a special connection, Melanie reminded herself. *Just like Christina and Star.*

She hoped that was true—and she hoped it would be enough to change everyone's minds about the pretty black filly.

6

"So what do you think of Tall Oaks?" Fredericka asked Monday morning as she and Melanie strolled down the stone walkway in front of Fredericka's home.

Sunday night Christina and Melanie had gotten home after midnight. Exhausted after the concert and the swimming, both girls had slept late. At eleven the next morning Ashleigh and Mike had dropped Melanie off at Fredericka's farm on their way into town. Whitebrook was hosting a Labor Day picnic for family, friends, and farm workers, and Mike and Ashleigh were buying last-minute ice and supplies. They were picking Melanie up on their way home.

"It's fantastic!" Melanie replied sincerely. Fredericka had just finished giving her a tour of the interior of the house, which dated back to the Civil War. It was a two-story brick structure with white columns and four chimneys.

Outside, the grounds were shaded with dogwoods, willows, and oaks, which were lush with green foliage. Rows of pink geraniums, purple peonies, and white petunias lined the walkways and dotted the mulched gardens.

"Tall Oaks has belonged to my family since the mid–1800s," Fredericka continued as she led Melanie down the walk. "Many homes in the area were burned during the Civil War. We were spared because my great-great-grandmother turned it into a hospital for soldiers and citizens with smallpox. It was such a contagious disease that the Union soldiers stayed far away."

As Fredericka talked, Melanie listened with interest, even though she was dying to see Image. Keeping her head tilted toward Fredericka so that she wouldn't seem rude, her eyes searched the grounds for the barn and pastures.

Fredericka must have noticed, because she laughed and said, "Here I am rattling on about my family's history when you're eager to see Image, who I must say is very happy to be home."

Fredericka led her up an oak-lined drive toward the stables.

"How long have you been raising horses?" Melanie asked as they walked, her heart speeding up at the thought of seeing Image once more.

"My family has a long history of breeding and racing Thoroughbreds," Fredericka explained as they walked to the red brick barn. Pillars framed the front entrance, so the barn matched the mansion. "Charles was very involved in the business, and when he died, I was determined to carry on. Fortunately, I was able to hire Alexis Huffman, a top-notch manager recommended to me by Brad Townsend."

Melanie winced. *Brad.* After the previous night, she'd had enough of him.

"Alexis worked in California for Ron Abrams," Fredericka continued. "Last year I was able to convince her to come east and be my farm manager. Since then she has been my right arm, advising me on everything. It's because of her that I have Gratis and my newest stallion, Khan." Her eyes shone. "Wait until you see him. He's magnificent, with excellent bloodlines. He's young, so I only bred him lightly this spring, but I have high hopes for his new foals."

When they reached the pillared entrance, Fredericka led Melanie inside. The double doors opened into a wide aisle that had a dozen stalls running down each side. Fans whirled overhead and shutters darkened the windows, keeping the interior cool. Each stall was labeled with a gold-lettered nameplate, and as they walked down the aisle Fredericka introduced each horse. Melanie was impressed that Fredericka knew the bloodlines of every broodmare, weanling, and yearling. Even though the farm wasn't as large as

Whitebrook, which had three barns, it was definitely first-class.

"This is Townsend Mistress," Fredericka said, stopping in front of a spacious stall. Melanie peered in, eager to see Image's dam. She had Image's beautiful face and glossy black coat, but her back was slightly swayed and her ribs and stomach were as round as a barrel—the way broodmares often looked after having lots of foals.

"So this is the mare that got away," Melanie murmured.

"What, dear?"

"I heard that Brad was angry he sold Mistress to you and that he wanted her back," Melanie explained.

Fredericka made a *tsk*ing sound. "Don't believe everything you hear. Ever since Charles died, Brad's been a prince."

Brad? A prince? Melanie choked back a snort of disbelief. If Brad was nice to Fredericka, it was because he wanted something—like his horse back.

"Is she in foal again?" Melanie asked as they continued down the aisle.

"No. Her last colt, Master Charles, named for my dear departed husband, was so big and demanding, he wore her out. She'll have a break this year, but I hope she'll be ready in the spring. I want to breed her to Khan. As you know, she has lovely babies."

Melanie halted in front of an empty stall that had Image's name written on it. A leather lead line hung from a brass hook, but the filly was nowhere in sight. Melanie turned to ask Fredericka where Image was, but the older woman had continued down the aisle.

At the end of the barn was a separate, modern wing. "Last year we built this addition for Khan—and for Gratis when he retires to stud. Khan has a spacious stall, paddock, washroom, and breeding area," Fredericka said, obviously proud of the new facility.

A deep whinny drew Melanie to Khan's stall. He was a powerfully built mahogany bay stallion with a white stripe down his nose.

"He's very handsome," she breathed.

"He's a descendant of Alydar," Fredericka said. "He raced three years on the West Coast, winning over three million dollars. Alexis convinced me to buy him and bring him east. She said his bloodlines would attract breeders from all over the world."

"Talking about me?" Melanie turned to see a tall, slender woman approach, a halter and chain lead shank in her gloved hand.

"Lexi, I'm glad you're here. I want to introduce you to Melanie Graham, who will be working with Image."

Melanie thought she saw a flash of annoyance in the woman's green eyes, but then Alexis smiled warmly. "Nice to meet you. I saw you ride Wonder's Star against Gratis in the Breeder's Futurity. You did a great job."

"Thank you." Alexis pulled off her gloves, and Melanie shook her hand, which was cool to the touch.

The farm manager didn't look much older than twenty-five, and though her walnut brown bob was casually pushed back behind her ears and her face was free of makeup, she looked pretty enough to be a model.

"So you're going to train Image, huh?" Lexi's tone was matter-of-fact, though Melanie thought she heard a hint of sarcasm in her voice. But she knew she had no reason to be so sensitive. It was already clear that everyone except Fredericka thought Image was untrainable.

"I'm going to try," Melanie said as confidently as she could. "I'd hate to see her end up a broodmare before she was even given a chance."

"Though she will make a lovely mate for Khan," Fredericka said.

Alexis opened the stallion's door. "I'm going to turn him out while the mares are inside," she said. Deftly she grabbed the stallion's halter and looped the lead chain over his nose. Melanie stepped back as Khan pranced out of his stall. He looked like a handful, but Alexis seemed unfazed.

Fredericka turned to Melanie. "Now I bet you're wondering where Image is."

"She isn't kept in the barn?"

Shaking her head, Fredericka linked her arm through Melanie's and followed Alexis and Khan outside. "No, she hates being cooped up. She has her own pasture with a run-in shed."

"She doesn't mind being alone?" Melanie asked. "That's unusual for horses."

Fredericka laughed. "Like I told you before, she thinks she's a person. Though she does have a friend with her."

Fredericka stopped in the shade of a tree and pointed down the hill to a rolling green pasture. Craning her neck, Melanie spotted Image grazing alongside a little mouse brown pony. No, not a pony, Melanie decided. Its ears were too long.

She wrinkled her nose. "A donkey?" she asked.

"That's Pedro. He's the only animal on the entire farm that will put up with Image's spoiled behavior."

Melanie laughed. When they reached the pasture, Image threw up her head. As soon as she saw Fredericka, she trotted over. With the backdrop of the tree-dotted hills and white board fence, the filly looked more beautiful than ever.

"How's my princess?" Fredericka crooned. She dug in the pocket of her sundress and brought out a handful of carrots. Image took them daintily from Fredericka's hand, then nuzzled her for more. Melanie could tell by the filly's expression that she was calmer and happier at the farm. This was definitely the place to start training, and Melanie fervently hoped that the filly would be less trouble than she had been at the track.

"What a sweet girl." Melanie stroked the filly's neck. Just then Pedro ambled over to see what was going on. Laying her ears back, Image shot the donkey such a vicious look that Melanie was amazed at the transformation.

"I'm afraid *sweet* might not be the right adjective," Fredericka said, sighing. Then she smiled at Melanie. "Are you going to start working with her today?"

"Yes—if that's okay with you. I'll work her in her pasture so that if she does get away, she'll be confined. *Not* that I'm planning on letting her get away," she added firmly.

Fredericka's smile grew broader and her eyes twinkled. "I have complete confidence in you, my dear." She patted Melanie's shoulder. "I'm going into Lexington. The last thing you need is me breathing down your neck. Alexis will be here if you need anything."

Melanie slid her hands into the back pockets of her jeans, suddenly feeling unsure. "Thanks. I'm going to try to work with her every day. I'll come in the afternoons unless schoolwork interferes. Would you like a daily report?"

"Weekly will be fine, though I do enjoy your company, Melanie, so I hope you'll stop in and visit often." Giving her shoulder one last pat, Fredericka went up the hill. Melanie waved good-bye, then turned back to the pasture. Image was still standing by the fence, watching her with interest.

Melanie's heart beat faster. This was it. Her chance to work with the horse of her dreams.

"We're going to have a great time," she told Image, hoping she sounded confident. She turned and jogged

65

up the hill to the barn, retrieving Image's lead line. Except for the broodmares, the barn was empty. Melanie breathed a sigh of relief. She didn't want an audience on the first day.

For this first session she'd lead Image around the pasture, working on making her walk quietly by her side, halt, and stand. If the filly was as smart as Melanie thought, she'd pick up voice commands quickly.

"Hey, girl," Melanie crooned when she opened the gate. Pedro had retreated to the shade of the run-in shed, but Image stood rooted next to the gate, as if waiting to see what would happen next.

"Ready for a little fun?" Melanie held out her hand, palm up. Image snuffled it, but as soon as Melanie reached for her halter, she backed up.

I'd better loop the rope around her neck first, Melanie decided. But when she moved toward her, Image again stepped back—just far enough so Melanie couldn't reach her.

"Oh, I get it. You think this is a game. Like tag." Image bobbed her head, and Melanie blew out her breath. No way could she win a game of tag with a horse who could run ten times as fast as she could.

Reaching down, she pulled up some grass. "How about a yummy treat?"

Image's ears flicked, and she stretched out her neck, but when Melanie pulled the grass closer, she danced away, shaking her head as if to say, *You're not fooling me again with that trick!*

"Fine." Frustrated, Melanie ran her fingers through her hair. The sun was beating on her head, and sweat beaded on her upper lip. *Next time I'll bring carrots,* she thought.

Racking her brain, Melanie tried to remember things she'd read about how to catch an evasive horse. *Don't chase the horse and don't give up without succeeding,* she recalled a magazine article saying. She also remembered reading about walking a horse down, which could take hours, and Mike and Ashleigh would be there soon to pick her up.

Melanie tapped her lip, her gaze swinging to Pedro. She remembered how furious Image had been when the donkey came over for attention. Maybe Pedro was the key.

"Hey, Pedro, come here, cutie pie," Melanie said. Walking across the pasture, she held out her hand. She didn't even have to look over her shoulder to tell that Image was following her. "I bet you're hot and itchy with all that fuzzy hair."

The donkey gazed at her with big, slanted eyes. Melanie went into the shed, put her arm around his neck, and began to scratch his withers. "Oh, I bet that feels good."

Image couldn't stand it. Striding up, she bumped Melanie with her muzzle as if to say, *What about me?*

Quickly Melanie slid the rope around Image's neck. While the filly was busy giving Pedro a get-lost look, Melanie slipped the halter over her head and snapped the lead to the ring. "There. Was that so bad?" Melanie asked, feeling her excitement rise—and all because she'd managed to catch a horse!

"I'm just going to have to be twice as smart as you." She scratched Image under the forelock and mane. When the filly wiggled her upper lip, Melanie laughed. "Getting caught wasn't so terrible, and learning new things will be fun, you'll see."

Holding the lead with both hands, Melanie said in a singsong voice, "Walk," then took several steps. Image followed like a lamb for two strides, then suddenly jumped sideways, throwing up her head at the same time. Instinctively Melanie gripped the lead tightly with both hands, dug in her heels, and braced herself, but when Image hit the end of the rope, the force jerked Melanie clean off her feet.

She flew through the air, landing flat on her stomach, and the breath blew out of her in a loud *oomph*. Snorting loudly, Image reared back on her haunches.

"Whoa!" Melanie declared, furious and determined *not* to let go of the lead. She couldn't let Image get away. She just couldn't!

With a toss of her head, Image danced backward. Melanie let out a grunt as she was yanked along the ground. Her T-shirt rode up, and her bare skin scraped against the grass.

Gripping more tightly, Melanie held on. *Be an anchor. Don't let go.*

Then Image wheeled and took off. Melanie held

fast, her fingers cramping on the rope and her elbows and knees burning as she thumped and banged across the field.

Tears streamed down her cheeks, and when the pain in her fingers grew too sharp and she could no longer hold on, she screamed with frustration—then let go.

Image raced across the pasture, the rope flying beside her. Confused, Pedro trotted from the shed. When Image reached the corner of the field, she slid to a stop, wheeled, and reared, her hooves pawing the air. Melanie held her breath, praying the filly wouldn't get tangled in the rope. When she dropped down and stood quietly, Melanie exhaled with relief.

Melanie bit her lip to stop the tears from falling. So much for her so-called connection with Image. How could she have been so stupid as to think she'd be able to train her when a respected trainer such as Vince Jones couldn't?

A triumphant neigh rang across the field.

Even Image was laughing at her.

7

"ARE YOU ALL RIGHT?"

Melanie turned her head. Alexis was leaning over the top fence board.

"I'm fine!" Melanie called as she struggled to her feet and assessed the damage. Raw patches dotted her stomach and elbows, her knees burned, and her fingers felt as if they were on fire.

"Just *fine*," she muttered, glancing over at Image, who had tired of the game and was calmly cropping grass.

Alexis opened the gate and walked into the pasture. Hands on her hips, she gave Melanie an assessing look. "You're in bad shape. You'd better let me catch her."

"I can do it," Melanie ground out through clenched teeth. Fingers curled into fists, she limped over to Image and planted her foot on the lead line, which trailed in the grass. Then she snatched up the rope, holding it gingerly in her sore hands.

"You think it's all a game, don't you?" Eyes narrowed, Melanie shook her finger at Image, who pricked her ears.

Melanie blew out a breath, her anger collapsing. If she was going to win the game, she'd have to outsmart Image, not bully her.

"Okay, you win this round," Melanie conceded. She stroked the filly's silky muzzle, then made her walk to the gate and halt. "There. That wasn't so hard." Melanie winced in pain. *No, it* was *hard—for me, anyway,* she thought.

"I'll be back," she added as she unsnapped Image's lead and stepped away.

Alexis opened the gate. Silently Melanie walked through and headed up the hill. She was too embarrassed to say anything.

"Want to come in the washroom and clean off those scrapes?" Alexis asked when they reached the barn. Melanie thought she heard a hint of smugness in the farm manager's voice, but her expression seemed sincere.

"No, thanks. My aunt and uncle should be here in a little while. I'll meet them at the end of the drive."

"Okay." Folding her arms, Alexis rocked back on her heels. "You know, you're wasting your time with Image. She's too smart, too spoiled, and too old. Maybe if you'd started working with her a year ago—"

Melanie held up her palm, which burned like fire. "Don't say it. I'm not giving up."

"But why bother?" Alexis asked. "She's not your horse. What's in it for you?"

Good question, Melanie thought. *Was* there anything in it for her? "I guess I just like her, that's all," she finally answered. "She needs someone to believe in her."

Alexis choked back a laugh. "And you're it?" she asked, pointing to Melanie's ripped T-shirt and grass-stained shorts. "Sorry," she apologized. "I find that kind of funny." Chuckling under her breath, she turned and went into the barn.

"I don't," Melanie muttered. Turning, she walked down the drive, trying not to limp. She didn't want Ashleigh flipping out when she saw her. Her aunt had just gotten over worrying about Christina's sprained wrist.

I'd better make up a story, Melanie decided as she stopped under a tree. Otherwise Mike or Ashleigh might forbid her to come back.

Fifteen minutes later the truck pulled up in the drive. Ashleigh opened the passenger door, her jaw dropping when she saw Melanie.

"I tripped over a bucket in the driveway," Melanie blurted before Ashleigh had a chance to say anything.

"You poor thing!" Ashleigh slid over to make room. Mike was craning his neck, trying to see around his wife.

"Those are some nasty scrapes, Mel," he declared. "We'd better get them cleaned up."

Biting her lip to keep from wincing, Melanie climbed into the truck. "It's nothing, really."

Ashleigh gently inspected Melanie's elbow. "These are deeper than you think. And there's dirt ground into them—and grass stains," she added, raising her eyes to meet Melanie's. "Would you like to tell us what really happened?" she asked gently.

Melanie turned away, a tear trickling down her cheek. "Okay, I didn't fall in the driveway." She told them the whole story.

"Melanie, are you sure you want to work with such an unruly horse? She's not even yours."

"I'm not going to give up, Aunt Ashleigh," Melanie said.

Ashleigh didn't say anything. Feeling miserable, Melanie stared out the window. All the way home Mike and Ashleigh talked about getting roughed up by horses. But Melanie didn't care about her cuts and bruises. What made her miserable was that she'd been so eager to have a relationship with a horse, she'd imagined some special connection with Image. A connection that clearly didn't exist.

Christina had raised Star from birth. Their close bond had taken two years to grow. Melanie had met Image twice. What had she expected?

The worst thing was that Melanie felt as if she'd failed Image somehow. She'd had a chance but blown it—big time. She'd told Image she'd be back. She'd told Alexis, Mike, and Ashleigh that she wouldn't give up. Who was she kidding—herself?

If Alexis told Fredericka what had happened, that would probably be the end of the training sessions. Maybe Image *would* be just as happy being a brood-mare. Bred to Khan, she'd live the rest of her life making beautiful foals. What was wrong with that?

She's the horse of my dreams. Melanie sighed. But she might as well face it: It had only been a dream.

"You're giving up? Just like that?" Christina snapped her fingers. She was sitting on the edge of the tub while it filled with hot water.

"No. Not just like that." Melanie inspected her wounds in the bathroom mirror. "I had the whole ride home to think about it."

"Mel, this weekend you were high as a kite over that horse. And now, after one training session—granted, a not too successful one—you're ready to quit? Where's the old Mel? The one who never gave up?"

"Hey, what's with the lecture?" Mel sputtered. "Are you my shrink? My spiritual guru?"

"No, I'm your cousin." Christina gave her a fierce look. "And I know you, Mel. I know something's been wrong ever since you took that fall on Fast Gun. All summer you've frantically thrown yourself into this jockey thing, but your heart's not in it."

Melanie opened her mouth, hoping some clever comeback would pop out, but she knew her cousin was on target. Picking up a washcloth, she dabbed at her elbows. "You're right," she admitted with a sigh. "When I first met Image, I thought I'd figured out what was wrong with me—what was missing. I wanted a horse to love the way you love Star. I wanted it so much, I got a little carried away."

"Or maybe you gave up too soon. Star and I have been together a long time."

"I know. I told myself all that. But it's kind of tough to love a horse that drags you through the mud and then laughs in your face."

"Yeah, but you know she can be sweet if she wants to be." Christina flexed her wrist. She wasn't wearing the bandage, but Melanie knew her wrist was still sore.

"How's Gratis doing?" Melanie asked, almost afraid to bring up the subject.

"He needed ten stitches, but his wound's healing nicely."

"Good. Has Vince forgiven Image?"

"Are you kidding?" Christina shook her head. "He calls her the bad luck filly."

Melanie held out her arms, which were starting to scab over. "She didn't exactly bring me good luck. Tomorrow's the first day of school, and I look like roadkill."

"Don't forget the twenty people coming over for Whitebrook's picnic later today," Christina said, trying to keep a straight face. "But don't worry. You always look a little weird. No one will notice the difference." She started to giggle.

"Gee, thanks." Miffed, Melanie threw the washcloth at her. It splatted in the middle of her cousin's chest, soaking her T-shirt.

"Hey! This is what I was going to wear to the party!" Sputtering, Christina threw the washcloth back, and they both burst out laughing.

Christina stood up. "Hurry up and take your bath so you can help me stuff those deviled eggs."

"Don't wait. I'm going to soak for a long time."

When Christina left, Melanie turned off the hot water. Christina was right. She couldn't give up on Image. The filly had too much potential. Melanie had expected too much too fast. Feeling better, Melanie pulled off her grass-stained clothes and got into the tub.

Half an hour later she was ready to join the party. She'd doctored up the scrapes on her arms and put on a loose, long-sleeved shirt and khaki pants to cover up her bruises.

When she went downstairs she could hear talking and laughing in the kitchen. Ian, Beth, and Kevin had arrived. Kevin had an armful of hot dog and hamburger buns in plastic bags, Ian was hoisting a cooler full of soda onto the porch, and Beth had just set a covered casserole onto the counter.

"Baked beans," she announced. "They'll need to stay warm in the oven."

When Kevin caught Melanie's eye, he smiled and asked, "How'd the training go?"

"Oh, just fine!" Melanie said too loudly as she hurried over to help Christina with the deviled eggs. Her cousin had gooey yellow stuff all over her hands and shirt.

"Do you need help, Chef Reese?" Melanie asked.

Christina wrinkled her nose. "Yes! I am so sick of this stuff." She held up a spoonful of yolk mixture. "Now I'm really going to have to change my clothes."

Laughing, Melanie took the spoon from her cousin and deftly plopped the yolk mixture into the eggwhite half. "*Voilà.*"

"Oh, go ahead, *brag*," Christina grumbled. She gave Melanie a sideways glance. "Aren't you going to tell Kevin what happened? He might be able to give you some suggestions on what to do with Image."

"Why would he bother talking to me?" Melanie asked. "Isn't *Lindsay* coming?"

There was an awkward silence.

Melanie glanced sharply at Christina. "She is coming, isn't she?"

"Well, um, yes. Parker's picking her up on his way over."

"Oh, great." Melanie dropped the spoon on the counter, and yolk splattered everywhere.

"Mel, it's been weeks since you and Kevin split up. I thought you were over it."

77

Melanie sighed. "I am. I just . . . well, I miss talking to him."

Christina nudged her with her elbow. "He's still your friend, Mel. He always will be."

"I know. You're right." Picking up the ruined egg, Melanie stuck it in her mouth. If she and Kevin were going to stay friends, she'd just have to get used to sharing him with girls like Lindsay Devereaux.

After washing her hands, Melanie went outside. Her aunt and uncle had moved several picnic tables under the shade of the backyard oak trees. A grill was heating, and a volleyball net was set up in the flat area. In the middle of the yard, two kids splashed in a big plastic swimming pool. Joe Kisner, one of the farm workers, was talking to Jonnie, another worker.

Melanie spotted Ian McLean coming out of the kitchen. The farm manager was wearing an apron that said STAND BACK—CHEF AT WORK. He was carrying a platter of hamburger patties and a metal spatula.

Melanie went over to talk to him. If anyone would know what to do with Image, Ian would.

"Hey, Mel, will you lift the lid off the grill for me?"

"Sure."

While Ian put the burgers on the grill, Melanie told him about Image. "Obviously I need help," she concluded.

"Spoiled rotten, huh?" Ian puffed out his cheeks. "They're the toughest. You can get rough with a stud

78

colt. Sometimes that's the only thing they respect. And the old-fashioned trainers would just beat the rottenness out of her. But I've found that if you get rough with a smart filly like Image, she'll turn sulky and mean. She won't run worth a lick for you, and one day you'll turn your back on her and wham! She'll nail you."

"Image isn't mean—yet. But she has the potential." Melanie remembered the look Image had given Pedro. "She just expects to get her own way, and so far she's gotten it."

"Then you have to be patient," Ian said. "If she's as smart as you say, she's going to get bored in a pasture all day. Intrigue her. Make friends with her. Get her on your side."

"I can do that." A grin spread over Melanie's face.

"Try working her in a smaller area. When you lead her, hug her side. If she tries to bolt, don't fight her. Go with her. Be her shadow. She'll soon figure out you're going to stick with her no matter what. And—" With a furtive look on his face, Ian checked to see if anyone was listening before adding, "Anytime she does what you want, give her a treat."

Melanie laughed. "So that's your secret all these years."

"There's no secret to good training. It's like raising kids—be patient and consistent." Ian's expression grew serious, and he pointed the spatula at Melanie. "At the same time, don't *ever* underestimate that filly.

And watch your back. You're working with a thousand-pound animal who can kill you with one swipe of her hoof."

Melanie nodded, her grin fading. "Thanks for the advice—and for being so graphic."

Ian chuckled. "Hey, it worked. You got my point. I don't want anyone getting hurt by a horse, especially someone I love like a daughter."

Melanie smiled. "Thanks, Ian."

"Melanie, will you help put the food out?" Ashleigh called from the open kitchen door.

Turning, Melanie waved acknowledgment. Parker and Lindsay were coming around the corner of the house. Lindsay had pulled her hair into a long ponytail, which swung from side to side as she walked. She had a volleyball under one arm and a bowl of something in her hand.

Melanie greeted the two, then took the bowl from Lindsay. "I'll put it on the picnic table."

"Thanks. It's Jell-O salad with fruit and those little marshmallows," Lindsay told her. "Kevin's favorite."

"That's his favorite?" Melanie asked in disbelief.

"Yeah." Lindsay glanced around. "Is Kevin here?"

"Um, I think he's in the kitchen."

"Thanks!"

Melanie watched her skip away up the porch steps. No wonder Kevin liked Lindsay, Melanie thought. Not only was she cute, friendly, popular, and one of the key players on the girls' varsity soccer team, but she knew what kind of dessert he liked! In fact, Lindsay and Kevin were the perfect match.

Melanie might as well admit it—there was no way she could compete. *Not that I want to try,* she decided. During the next few weeks she wouldn't have time even to *think* about Kevin. From now on, she was concentrating on Image.

She remembered Alexis's questions: "Why bother? What's in it for you?"

Melanie wasn't sure what the answers were. All she knew was that there was something unique about Image, something only she—and Fredericka—could see. Something that made her smile whenever she thought about the beautiful, spirited filly.

Ian was right. She had to be patient. And Christina was right, too.

Melanie couldn't give up.

8

"WHY DOES THE FIRST DAY OF SCHOOL SEEM TO LAST FOR-
ever?" Melanie grumbled to Christina as they walked
down the crowded hallway at Henry Clay High. The
two girls were on their way to their last-period class,
driver education. Since Christina took all honors
classes, it was the only one they shared.

Christina laughed. "Forever? We've only been here
since ten-thirty."

This summer the girls, Ashleigh, and Mike had met
with the advisors at school to work out a special schedule. Their first class didn't start until third period. That
way they could continue to exercise-ride at Whitebrook or the racetrack in the mornings.

"It seems like it," Melanie said. "I can't wait to get
to Tall Oaks so I can work with Image. This time I'm
taking gloves and treats and—"

"Mel! Chris! Wait up!" Melanie turned to see Katie Garrity jogging down the hall toward them. She was grinning from ear to ear. "I've got driver ed with you guys. Isn't that cool?"

"Awesome!" Melanie said. She and Christina had seen Katie only a few times all summer. When the girls were younger, they'd taken riding lessons together at Gardener Farm. Later Melanie and Christina had started to exercise-ride and race, and Katie had gotten involved with the school band and drama club.

"We can drive Mr. Hamrick crazy." Melanie made a steering motion with one hand. "Get it?"

Christina rolled her eyes. "We get it, Mel."

As they went into the classroom Katie was still grinning so happily that Melanie had to ask, "I know you're not this excited about driver ed. What's up?"

"You know the school's putting on the musical *Grease* this year," Katie said. "Tryouts were last Friday, before school started, and today they announced the parts. I got the role of Sandy!"

Grabbing Katie's hand, Christina hopped up and down. "Yes!"

Still talking, Christina sat down in the middle of a row of seats, and Katie sat next to her. Melanie took a seat behind her cousin. The room was half filled with students. Melanie recognized faces, but since she spent so little time at school, she didn't know many names.

"So who got the part of Danny Zucko?" Christina asked in a low voice.

"Tony Bianco," Katie whispered.

"Tony?" Christina repeated. "Talk about type-casting."

Tony rode a motorcycle to school every day and never took off his leather jacket.

"Yeah, well, you should hear him sing. And he can dance." Katie got a dreamy look on her face. Melanie and Christina exchanged glances. "Uh-oh," they chorused.

"Don't tell me you've got a crush on him," Melanie teased.

"Girls." Mr. Hamrick's voice boomed across the room. "The bell has rung."

Melanie turned her attention to Mr. Hamrick, who had a shiny, bald head and wore ties with Looney Tunes characters on them. "This is your senior year," Mr. Hamrick said while he passed out manuals. "Your last year at Henry Clay—I *hope*," he added, casting his gaze around the room.

Melanie cringed even though he hadn't been looking at her. Okay, so her grades junior year hadn't been too hot, but she hadn't flunked anything.

"Driver ed is only one semester, unless you fail the written test—or crash the car. In that event, you'd have to take the course again next semester." As he continued to tell them what to expect, Melanie's mind wandered.

She was glad she was finally going to take driver ed, and she wanted to do well so that she could get her license, but she had trouble paying attention in any class. Academics were not her strength, and she'd never really fit in at school. But sometimes, like when Katie chattered on about the class play, she felt sad about all the things she'd missed. She'd never joined a club, played a sport, run for an office, or stayed after school to . . . well, to do anything. Under her yearbook picture would be a big blank space.

This year would be her last chance to get involved in any activities that Henry Clay had to offer. Biting her lip, Melanie wondered if there was anything she might want to do. Paint scenery for the play? Go out for intramural volleyball? Join the ski club?

Nope. All she wanted was to see Image again that afternoon.

Melanie had arranged to have the school bus drop her off at Tall Oaks every day after school. That afternoon she jogged up the long drive to the house, leaving her backpack and her school shoes on Fredericka's porch. Then she headed for the barn.

Melanie's pockets bulged with carrot slices. She wore a baseball cap, gloves, jeans, and a determined expression. She had a currycomb under one arm and a lead rope slung over her shoulder.

"You look ready for war," Alexis said when Melanie came up the driveway to the barn. The farm manager was holding the lead line of a chestnut colt in one hand and was hosing off the horse's swollen knee with the other.

"Bone chip?" Melanie guessed, nodding toward the colt.

"Yeah. He had surgery two weeks ago. We're hoping he'll be able to race again."

"At Whitebrook, we use those new ice boots to—"

Alexis shot her such a cold look that Melanie stopped in midsentence. "Thanks," the farm manager said. "But I know what I'm doing."

Well, excuse me. Ducking her head, Melanie hurried into the barn.

"Hi!" Elizabeth greeted her. She was brushing a young gray filly hooked to crossties. "Image is waiting for you."

"Thanks." Melanie stopped to pat the yearling. "Who's this?"

"Crystal. Fredericka bought her last month. Alexis spotted her at another farm and decided she'd be a good addition."

Melanie scrutinized the filly's straight legs, well-angled shoulders, and intelligent eye. "Alexis has good taste."

"Yeah." Elizabeth glanced down the aisle toward the entrance, then added in a low voice, "Expensive taste, too. This filly cost Fredericka almost half a million dollars."

Melanie's eyes grew round. Spending half a million dollars on a yearling wasn't that unusual, but most of the expensive horses were bought by syndicates, meaning they were owned by several people. Melanie hadn't realized Fredericka was wealthy enough to pay that kind of money for one filly.

"How much did she pay for Khan?" Melanie asked, keeping her voice low, too. Obviously Elizabeth didn't want to get caught gossiping about her boss.

"More. A lot more. I heard hints that Fredericka took a second mortgage on Tall Oaks to pay for him."

Melanie gave a low whistle. The sudden clomp of hooves on concrete made Elizabeth and Melanie jump.

"Elizabeth, are you done with Crystal?" Alexis asked sharply as she came in, leading the chestnut horse.

"Uh, almost," Elizabeth mumbled. Scurrying around Crystal, she gave Melanie a don't-say-a-word look.

"Elizabeth was telling me another Image story," Melanie fibbed.

"Right. I was telling her about the time she bit the blacksmith in the butt and ripped a big hole in his pants."

"I would have loved to see that," Melanie said with a laugh. Alexis stared at the girls disapprovingly, and Melanie decided it was time to leave. She began to back down the aisle. "Well, gotta go."

Nickering at Melanie as if they were long-lost buddies, Image met her at the gate. Pedro stood in the run-in shed, switching at flies with his stubby tail.

"So you remember me?" Melanie asked, setting the brush on top of a fence post. "I guess it must have been a whole lot of fun dragging me around yesterday, huh?"

Stopping in front of the gate, Melanie made a big deal about pulling out a piece of carrot. "Ooh, look what I found. Your favorite treat. Only you're not getting one unless I catch you."

She opened the gate, latched it behind her, and held out the carrot. When Image tried to take it, Melanie pulled it out of reach. Still holding out the carrot, Melanie turned so that she was beside Image's neck. Image took the carrot the same instant Melanie snapped the lead onto the halter with her right hand.

"There. That was easy." Melanie stroked the filly's neck, taking a minute to savor her beauty. She was covered in a layer of dirt from rolling, but Melanie could still see patches of her glossy black coat. "Let's get you cleaned up. I bet you like being pampered, little princess."

Holding on to the lead, Melanie began to curry the filly's dusty coat. Dirt and hair flew everywhere. Image twitched and wriggled, but Melanie kept slack in the rope and moved with her.

"Just call me your shadow," Melanie told her, recalling what Ian had said. Whenever Image stood quietly, Melanie praised her, and when they were all done, she fed her some carrot slices. "Now, the next time I come, you'll remember me as the carrot person, not the person you dragged around."

Unsnapping the lead, Melanie stepped back. Image just stood there, bobbing her head as if to say, *Is that all?*

Happiness rose in Melanie's throat. Okay, so fifteen minutes of grooming was a long way from breezing a furlong at the track.

But it was a start.

Saturday morning Melanie galloped Rascal along the inside railing at Whitebrook. After the hectic Labor Day weekend races, Mike and Ashleigh had decided not to race the next weekend, so the horses in training had easy workouts.

Later that day Christina would be going to the track to race a horse for Vince and a horse for June Fortig. No one had asked Melanie to ride, and she hadn't felt like hanging around the track that morning to hustle mounts for the day's races. She'd rather spend her time with Image.

Melanie balanced lightly in the saddle, the wind brushing against her cheeks. The sun was rising, and the air was cooler than it had been the last couple of days. Rascal's stride was as comfortable and even as the motion of a rocking chair, and Melanie found herself relaxing and thinking about Image.

Their sessions together Wednesday, Thursday, and Friday had been terrific. The filly had loved being groomed, and at the end of each lesson Melanie had led her around the pasture, rewarding her with treats. Since they would have more time this afternoon, Melanie was going to put her light racing saddle on Image's back, just to let her get the feel of it. If that was successful, the next step would be the bridle. And then longe lines and then . . . Goose bumps prickled Melanie's arms at the thought of being the first person on Image's back.

When they had cantered past the finish line, Melanie slowed Rascal to a trot. He jogged halfway around the oval, then broke into a walk. His neck was sweaty, but when Melanie laid her palm on it, it felt cool to the touch.

As they walked back toward the break in the fence, Melanie watched Christina gallop past on Star. The handsome colt had recovered completely from his grueling mile-and-a-half race the previous Saturday. In fact, Melanie thought, he'd never looked better. His ears were alert; his stride ate up the track. Christina was rating him, but Melanie could tell his time was still fast.

Obviously Melanie wasn't the only one who thought the colt looked strong. Brad, Ashleigh, and Mike were lined up along the fence, watching the chestnut colt go. Mike and Brad both had stopwatches. Ashleigh was jotting down notes in the little notebook she always carried.

When she rode Rascal closer, Melanie could hear them talking.

"Turfway doesn't have any decent races until October," Brad was saying. "The top trainers are taking their horses to New York, where the big purses are. Star's ready. If we're thinking of him as a Derby contender, then we've got to start racing him on other tracks against the top competition."

Melanie could tell by the expressions on Mike's and Ashleigh's faces that they were seriously considering Brad's suggestion. Whitebrook hadn't had a horse like Star since Wonder's Pride had won the Kentucky Derby and the Preakness. They wanted to make sure they did things right.

Melanie rode Rascal through the gap in the track fence, where Dani Martens met her. "How'd he go?" the groom asked, taking the reins.

"As smooth as always," Melanie said as she dismounted. "He's not even hot."

When Dani led Rascal away, Melanie walked over to stand beside Ashleigh. Her aunt was showing a leaflet to Mike. "Here is a list of upcoming races at Belmont." She tapped the page with her finger. "In two weeks there are at least two races that would be perfect for Star."

Just then Christina rode up. Her face was flushed under her helmet, and she was breathing hard. Star wasn't even winded. "He could've run another mile!" Christina gasped as she slid off.

"That's just what we were discussing, Chris. Belmont's got a mile-and-a-half Grade I race for two- and three-year-old colts," Ashleigh said. "It would be the perfect distance for Star."

"Belmont? What are you talking about?" Christina asked. Pulling the reins over Star's head, she led the colt through the gap.

"Taking Star to New York."

Christina frowned. "New York? That's so far away."

Ashleigh laughed. "Hey, don't look so glum. You'd come, too—to be Star's jockey."

"Me? Ride at Belmont?" Christina's eyes grew huge. Riding at the prestigious track, one of the oldest in the United States, had always been a dream for both Melanie and Christina.

"All right, Chris!" Raising her hand, Melanie slapped palms with Christina.

Brad opened his mouth as if to protest, and Ashleigh glanced at him in warning.

"That would be part of the deal," Ashleigh said firmly. "If Star goes to New York, Christina will ride him. Right, Brad?"

"I suppose," Brad agreed reluctantly.

"Wait a minute," Mike cut in, looking a little skeptical. "We'd have to take Star up at least five days before the race. And right now we don't have any other horses ready for that class of races. That means we'd tie up the van, a groom, and a driver, all for one horse."

"No problem," Brad said. "Vince Jones is taking several horses to New York. I've already asked him if he has room for Star, and he said he does." He looked expectantly at Mike, then Ashleigh. When a smile filled Ashleigh's face, Melanie knew that her aunt was all for it.

"Sounds good to me," Mike said, putting his arm around Ashleigh's shoulders.

Christina and Melanie whooped with excitement, startling Star, who tossed his head and snorted loudly.

Ashleigh hugged Mike around the waist. "We'll make a vacation of it. We haven't seen Cindy in ages, and Mel, we can get Susan and your dad to drive out to the track, or we can go into the city to meet them. It'll be so much fun."

"It will be," Melanie said, as excited as Christina. Okay, so she was a little jealous she wouldn't be riding, but she'd get over it. After all, it was a chance to see her dad, to meet Cindy McLean, Ian and Beth's daughter, who was a jockey in New York, and to hobnob with a lot of hotshot trainers and jock she'd only read about.

But then she thought about ___e. It would mean she wouldn't get to ___with ___ filly for several days. ___ool is that?"

___iled back. The trip w___d be fun, and she__ but she wouldn't be gone that long. She would miss ___seen her dad in so lon___ "New York, here we come!" she cried.

93

9

EYES AIMED STRAIGHT AHEAD, MELANIE DROVE DOWN THE road, her fingers tightly gripping the steering wheel of the Reeses' car. She was going at least ten miles under the speed limit, but still felt as if the car were speeding. Behind her someone honked. She glanced in the rearview mirror, wincing when she saw a car right on her bumper.

"Ignore them," Mike said from the passenger seat. He was clutching the dashboard, his knuckles white. It was Saturday afternoon. "Mike had suggested her drive to Oaks. "Take Frederick's way, so flip on your right-hand turn signal," Mike instructed, frowning in concentration. She knew the treated, down."

"Uh, right-hand turn signal," Meal and slow-was the thing sticking out on the left side of the steal ing wheel, but she couldn't remember whether to push it up or down.

"Mel, that's Fredericka's drive," Mike said, frantically pointing. "Slow down!"

Melanie stomped on the brake, and the car slammed to a halt. Tires screeched, and then the car behind her zoomed past in the other lane, its motor roaring.

"Get a bike!" the kid in the passenger seat yelled at her through the rolled-down window.

"Get an IQ!" Melanie hollered back, but the car had already disappeared around the curve.

Mike rolled his eyes. Sweat was beading on his forehead. "Concentrate, Melanie. Push the turn signal up, then slowly step on the gas and turn to the right."

"Got it." Melanie turned wide, and the car bounced over something hard at the edge of the drive.

Horrified, she looked over her shoulder to see what she'd run over.

"Aagh!" Mike grabbed the steering wheel as the car swerved onto the grass and headed for the white board fence that bordered both sides of the drive. "Step on the brake. Stop the car!"

Melanie braked inches from the fence.

"Melanie, you cannot take your eyes off the road!" Mike gasped.

"But I was afraid I ran over a turtle. It's just a rock, though, painted white. I don't know why Fredericka has them there—they're in the way."

Mike let out one long breath. "So people don't drive on her grass?"

"Oh." Melanie gave her uncle a weak smile. "I didn't do so hot, did I?"

"No worse than Christina. She has a little trouble judging distances, too. Now, do you think you can get up the drive without hitting the fence?"

"Sure." Melanie stepped on the gas. The motor revved, but the car didn't move. "You have to take it out of park," Mike suggested.

"Right. I knew that." Melanie carefully drove up to the barn. When she passed the turnoff to Fredericka's house, she noticed at least a dozen cars parked in front. "She must be having a party or something."

"Stop here." Mike waved to the right, where the drive widened into a turnaround. Beside the barn, under the shade of an oak tree, Elizabeth was cleaning halters. "I'll pick you up in an hour."

Melanie opened the car door. "Can I drive home, too?"

"We'll see," Mike said. She could tell by his pained expression that he'd rather drive himself.

Melanie pulled her exercise saddle, girth, and pad from the backseat of the car, then said good-bye to Mike. Elizabeth waved, and Melanie went over to where the groom was sitting on an overturned bucket, a pile of leather halters and a pail of water at her feet.

"You drove? Cool!" Elizabeth exclaimed.

"It's actually kind of fun. I can't wait to get my license so I can drive myself around."

"I've got my license, but sometimes I still have to bum rides," Elizabeth said. "I'm saving for a down payment on a car, but it's taking forever." She glanced at the saddle in Melanie's arms. "Is that for Image?"

"Yeah. I want to try setting it on her back to see what she does. She's been so good, I think we can move to the next step. Hey, what's going on up at the house?"

"Fredericka's having a lovely tea on the terrace," Elizabeth said in a mock English accent.

"Sounds ducky, love," Melanie responded, and the two girls laughed. "Well, I don't have much time, so I'd better get going."

As she hurried through the barn Melanie checked to see if Alexis was around. As usual, everything was spotless. From what Melanie could tell, the farm manager had a great eye for horses and did a terrific job. Still, Melanie always breathed a sigh of relief when she wasn't there to watch her with eagle eyes.

After grabbing a lead rope and a grooming bucket from the tack room, Melanie passed through the stallion wing to visit briefly with Khan before heading down the hill. Image and Pedro were under a tree, dozing out of the afternoon sun. Melanie whistled, and the filly trotted over.

"Are you happy to see me?" Melanie asked as she set the saddle on the top fence board. "Or is it the car-

97

rots?" Not that she cared. As long as Image kept learning and cooperating, Melanie would be happy.

Whistling a lively tune, Melanie groomed the filly until she glistened. Then she wiped her off with fly spray and picked out her hooves. Image seemed to love being fussed over, and when Melanie had finished brushing out her mane and tail, the filly shook her head and swished her tail as if to show them off.

Stepping back, Melanie admired her handiwork, and her heart swelled with pride at how much she'd accomplished in one week. Not only did Image seem to look forward to her visits, but Melanie thought the filly trusted her.

"I'm so glad I didn't give up," she whispered, running her hand down Image's silky neck. "Now, are you ready to try something new? After all, if you're going to become my famous racehorse—" Flushing, Melanie caught herself. "I mean *Fredericka's* famous racehorse, then you're going to have to get used to a saddle and bridle."

Picking the saddle off the top board of the fence, she held it under Image's muzzle. "See? It barely weighs anything. And this is the girth." She waved it in the air. "Here's the pad. Smells like Rascal, doesn't it?"

Melanie set the saddle back on the fence, then flapped the pad in the air, her heartbeat speeding up when Image sidled away from it. When the filly halted and turned to look at her curiously, Melanie immediately fed her a carrot and praised her.

After rubbing the pad all over the filly, Melanie finally slid it onto her back. "Now let's try the saddle." Keeping the lead line slack, Melanie placed the saddle gently on top of the pad. The filly's eyes rolled. Bending her neck around, she touched her side with her muzzle as if to ask, *What is that thing?*

Melanie held her breath, letting it out when Image's head swung back, her ears flicked forward, and she butted Melanie with her nose. Melanie smiled with relief. She wanted to jump up and down and holler, "Whoopee!" Instead she told Image what a perfect girl she was and that soon they'd be breezing on the racetrack, leaving all the naysayers in the dust.

"But first let's try tightening the girth. Just a notch," Melanie added as she buckled the girth on the saddle's right side. Going around to the left side, she reached under the filly's belly. "The saddle won't work if it isn't buckled on," she said in a singsong voice.

Slowly she drew the girth up and around, holding it in place. Pedro ambled from under the tree and began to eat. Image stood quietly, seeming more concerned about what Pedro was doing than the feel of the girth. Melanie raised the flap of the saddle and buckled the girth on the lowest hole.

The explosion was so fierce and unexpected it knocked Melanie off her feet.

Head tucked between her forelegs, Image twisted and whirled like a black tornado. With a squeal of anger, she charged across the field, bucking so hard Melanie felt the ground vibrate beneath her.

Her heart pounding, Melanie stood up. She had been to the rodeo only once, but she was positive that Image could outbuck any of the broncos she'd seen.

In a blur of movement Image galloped past, skidded into the corner, and reared. With a yelp, Melanie leaped onto the fence. "Whoa, easy," she called, her mouth dry with fear. What if Image crashed into a tree and hurt herself? What if she tripped on the lead line and went down?

But Image seemed to know exactly what she was doing. She flew across the pasture, chased Pedro into a corner, and then raced back again. When the saddle didn't come off, she slid to a stop and shook like a dog. Then she snaked her head around and began to bite at it.

"Hey! That's an expensive saddle!" Melanie hollered, waving her arms.

Snapping her head up, Image glared at Melanie, then took off again—straight for the pasture fence.

"No! Stop!" Melanie screamed as the filly charged toward the fence. A stride before it, Image leaped, narrowly clearing the top board.

Melanie blinked, not believing her eyes, then jumped off the fence. Image raced up the hill, disappearing into the barn. Melanie pounded after her. She could hear the clatter of hooves on concrete. Several horses whinnied, but by the time Melanie reached the barn, Image was trotting out the other side.

Elizabeth burst from the tack room. "What's going on?"

"Image is loose," Melanie called over her shoulder. When she reached the end of the barn, she ran onto the driveway. A car had just pulled up. Alexis climbed out, her expression furious. "How did that horse get loose?"

But Melanie didn't have time to answer. Image was flying across the lawn, nimbly dodging bushes and trees. As Melanie tore after her she bit back a sob. What if Image hurt herself?

Just then the saddle began to slip sideways. Image kicked high with both hind legs, leaped over a hedge, and disappeared around the corner of the house.

Melanie raced across the lawn. When she reached the corner, she heard several shrill screams. *Fredericka's party!* There was a loud crash of plates and glasses and more screaming.

She rounded the corner, skidding to a halt, and her mouth fell open. Women in summer hats and floral-print dresses were scattered everywhere. Tables and chairs were overturned, and broken dishes and spilled food and drinks lay strewn across the terrace.

Fredericka was helping an elderly woman who had fallen. When she caught sight of Melanie, she waved toward the other side of the house. "Image ran around that way!"

Melanie spun and headed to the front lawn, almost crashing into Alexis and Elizabeth. "I'll catch her," she shouted breathlessly. "You'd better help Fredericka and her guests."

By the time Melanie reached the front of the house, Image was racing down the grassy edge alongside the fence that bordered the drive. Melanie inhaled sharply. She was headed for the road!

Arms pumping, Melanie ran as hard as she could, but Image was too fast. There was no way she could catch her in time. She was going to run into the road. She was going to get hit!

Just then a pickup truck zoomed into the drive, braked, and drove forward and back inside the farm gates until it blocked the entrance to the driveway. Image careened to a stop, wheeled, and came bounding back toward Melanie.

Quickly Melanie plucked a carrot from her pocket. Holding out her hand, she planted herself in the middle of the galloping filly's path. "Whoa, girl," she called in a calm voice, though her heart was beating double time. "I've got a carrot!"

Image pricked her ears but didn't slow. Melanie stood her ground. At the last second the filly slid to a stop. Nostrils flared, eyes wide with excitement, she raised her head and blew loud puffs in the air. Then she dropped her nose and greedily devoured the carrot.

Melanie grabbed the lead line. Her arms and legs trembled from fatigue and relief. Her lower lip quivered. After patting Image's sweat-soaked neck, she glanced over her shoulder to see whose fast thinking had saved the filly's life. A redheaded boy dressed in a soccer jersey and shorts was jogging up the drive. Kevin.

"Melanie! Are you all right?" His freckled face was flushed under his baseball cap. Stopping beside her, he put his hand on her arm.

Melanie's mouth was so dry, she could only nod. She licked her lips, then swallowed. "Yes, thanks to you," she croaked. "I need to—" She gestured toward the saddle, which had slipped under Image's belly.

Kevin walked around to the other side and undid the girth. Melanie caught the saddle before it fell to the ground.

Alexis ran up and took the lead line from Melanie. On the front lawn of the house, a small crowd of women had gathered. Melanie spotted Fredericka with them.

"I'll take her," Alexis said, her tone so icy that Melanie flinched. "She needs cooling off."

Without another word, Alexis led Image up the drive. As Melanie watched them go, her eyes filled with tears. Kevin put his arm around her, and for a moment she sobbed into his jersey.

"I—I thought she was going to run into the road," she choked out. "I thought she'd be killed!"

"It's okay." Kevin stroked her hair. "It turned out okay."

Melanie shook her head. Leaning back, she looked up at him. "It's *not* okay. I blew it, Kevin. *Really* blew it."

Arm still around her shoulder, Kevin steered Melanie to his truck. "Tell me what happened."

Melanie dried her tears on the sleeve of her T-shirt. As they walked she told him about the last few days. "I thought she was ready for the saddle," she explained. "That was my first mistake."

"As far as I can tell, that was your only mistake. Mel, Image jumped a five-foot fence. There was no way you could have prevented that."

Melanie snorted. "Come on, Kevin. You're just being nice. You saw the way Alexis looked at me—like I was dirt. No, *worse* than dirt."

"Manure?" Kevin suggested, and Melanie couldn't help but laugh.

Melanie hopped into the passenger side of the truck. "All I want to do is go home and never show my face at Tall Oaks again," she said when Kevin got in on the driver's side.

"But you know you'd better explain to Fredericka what happened."

"I know. I need to apologize, too. But after that fiasco, I'll never be able to set foot on the farm again." Melanie heaved a sigh, then smiled weakly at Kevin. "I'm sure glad you showed up. Did I say thank you?"

"Ten times."

Kevin backed around, then drove up the drive. Fredericka was walking toward the house with several of her guests. "Let me out here," Melanie said, wiping her nose one last time.

"I'll go check on Image," Kevin said.

"Okay. I'll meet you in the barn."

Reluctantly Melanie climbed from the truck. Fredericka had ushered her friends inside the house and was waiting on the front porch. By the time Melanie reached the porch, fresh tears were gathering in her eyes. "I'm so sorry, Fredericka," she said.

"Well, that was quite scary." Fredericka pressed her hand over her heart. "For a moment I thought we had lost my princess. It was lucky that young man drove up when he did. The nick of time, I'd say."

"That's Kevin, Ian McLean's son," Melanie said, the tears spilling over.

Fredericka handed her a tissue. "There, there," she said in a soothing voice. "It's all over. Everything's all right."

"It's not all right." Melanie blew her nose. "I almost got Image killed, Fredericka."

"And how was it your fault?"

Melanie told her everything.

"Well, it sounds to me as if you did nothing wrong," Fredericka said. "Horses in training need to get used to the saddle. Image chose to behave like a wild monster and leap from the pasture." She waved her hand in an arc, emphasizing the word *leap*.

Melanie stared at Fredericka. "But Image got away from me. She busted up your entire party! Knocked over your guests! How can you not be mad at me?"

"Yes, she did rather crash my party, didn't she?" Leaning closer, Fredericka whispered, "But I must confess that until then it was terribly boring." She chuckled, then her expression turned serious. "Though we are going to have to make some changes before Image's next training session."

Linking her arm with Melanie's, she started up the drive to the barn. "I've already thought about it. I'm going to have a round pen built with a fence at least eight feet high. Alexis had suggested building one for working the babies, but it sounds as if Image needs it right now. Then I'm going to keep the gate closed at the end of the driveway. We don't want any other loose horses running into the road, now, do we? Can you think of anything else we could do before you work with her again?"

"You mean you'll *let* me work with her again?" Melanie asked, astonished.

"Of course, dear. I've been keeping an eye on you and Image. My princess likes you. I can tell."

Slipping her arm from Fredericka's, Melanie turned to face the older woman. She was amazed and glad that Fredericka wasn't mad at her, but she knew what she had to do. She couldn't live with herself if anything happened to Image.

"Thank you for not being furious with me, Fredericka," Melanie said, her heart growing heavy. "But I can't work with Image anymore. This has made me realize I don't know enough to train her. If something else happened and she was hurt, I would never forgive myself. I'm sorry," she added, choking out the last words. And before she started crying again, she fled up the drive to Kevin's truck.

10

MELANIE WAS SILENT DURING THE RIDE HOME. KEVIN KEPT glancing over at her, but she was too upset to talk. Pulling off the main road, Kevin stopped at a fast-food restaurant. "Come on, I'll treat you."

"I *am* hungry," Melanie admitted. After they ordered their food, Melanie went into the rest room to wash her hands. When she looked in the mirror, she gaped in horror. Her short hair stuck up in messy spikes, and dirt smudged her cheeks.

Quickly she washed her face and hands and finger-combed her hair. Feeling only slightly better, she slipped into the booth opposite Kevin, who was squirting ketchup on his double-decker cheeseburger.

Melanie finished her fish sandwich, then let out a satisfied sigh. Slumping back in the booth, she watched Kevin polish off the last of his fries. "Did I thank you yet for saving Image?" she teased.

"Yes, but you can thank me again."

Melanie laughed. "How did you just happen to be driving past Tall Oaks at that exact moment?"

"I finished soccer practice and decided to come see you."

"See me?"

He nodded. Dipping several fries in ketchup, he pointed them at her. "I wanted to see that perfect filly you've been raving about."

Melanie groaned under her breath. "Well, you saw her, all right."

"I did. And she's everything you said: powerful, balanced, intelligent—and really fast."

Melanie arched one brow. "Are you mocking me?"

"No," Kevin protested. "I had a chance to study her while Alexis hosed her off. Image was dancing on the end of the lead line as though she'd just won the Derby. She was barely winded and still trying to get her own way. And that look in her eye—it was challenging and proud."

As Kevin talked about the filly, Melanie held her breath, enraptured. "Then you see it, too!" she said excitedly when Kevin finished talking.

"Yeah. Great potential."

Melanie's shoulders slumped. "Too bad all she'll ever be is a broodmare."

"Did Fredericka actually say you couldn't work with her anymore?"

"No. Fredericka was all ready to build a round pen

for our next session. I was the one who said I wouldn't work with her anymore." Leaning forward, Melanie slapped her palms on the table. "It was stupid of me to think that I could train a horse like Image all by myself."

"So you're giving up?" Kevin asked, his tone matter-of-fact.

"I just realized that I don't have the experience—or the strength—to handle Image. Next time she could break a leg or crash through the fence."

"That's called giving up."

Melanie fumed. "It is not."

"Is too."

She threw her balled-up napkin at him.

"How about if I helped?" Kevin looked directly into her eyes, and Melanie knew he wasn't joking.

"But you have soccer and homework and scholarships and—Lindsay."

"True. But I could help on Saturdays and Sundays."

Melanie sucked in her breath, afraid to say anything.

"If you don't work with her," Kevin continued, "no one will. Image will be bred next year and every year after. She'll get swaybacked and ewe-necked, the gleam in her eyes will dim, and soon no one will remember how magnificent she was."

"Wow," Melanie breathed. "You're right, Kevin, but Image is so unpredictable and strong. Do you think I— we—have a chance?"

Kevin shrugged. "Not if you give up."

Melanie gnawed on her bottom lip. She took a long sip of her soda, mulling over everything Kevin had said.

Hope welled in her chest. Maybe she couldn't do it alone, but with Kevin's help . . .

Reaching across the table, Melanie grabbed Kevin's hand. A smile lit up her face. "You're right. Let's go for it."

That night at dinner Christina told Ashleigh, Mike, and Melanie about her second place that afternoon on High Five, one of the colts Vince Jones trained.

"Vince was really happy with second place," she said as she grabbed a piece of fried chicken. "But you know Vince—he was as grumpy as ever. It was the owner who came up to me and said that it was the first time High Five had even placed."

"Well done, Chris," Mike said. "Now if you and Melanie can only learn to drive as well as you ride! Christina missed two stop signs on the way home from the track," he told Ashleigh.

"That's because I was so excited," Christina said, beaming happily. "Mel, Vince wants me to ride Gratis at Belmont!"

"Wow!" Melanie dropped her forkful of salad. "Soon you'll be as famous as Julie Krone!"

Christina flushed. "No way. But I will get to ride two races on two great horses."

110

"I'm so proud of you, Chris!" Ashleigh smiled at her daughter. "It's about time Vince Jones recognized what a terrific jockey you are. Now if only Brad would notice."

"Ha." Christina snorted. "That'll be the day that horses fly."

Melanie laughed. If Christina had seen Image racing down Fredericka's drive, she would have sworn she *was* flying. When the three started talking about the trip to New York, Melanie's thoughts strayed to the filly. As soon as Kevin had brought Melanie home, she'd called Fredericka. After apologizing again, she'd told her about Kevin's offer to help and asked her if she still wanted her to work with Image. Without hesitating, Fredericka had said yes.

Melanie had planned to tell the Reeses about what had happened at Tall Oaks, since sooner or later they'd hear about it from Fredericka. But as the family chattered on about Belmont, going to a Broadway play, and seeing Cindy, she changed her mind. Melanie didn't want to push her luck. Her aunt and uncle could forbid her to work with the filly—or even worse, call her father, who would *not* be understanding.

After dinner Melanie helped Christina with the dishes.

"I've got to hurry. Katie's coming over," Christina said as she opened the dishwasher and stuck silverware in the basket. "She wants me to help her with her lines for *Grease*. She has pages and pages to memorize."

"You're not going out with Parker tonight?"

"No. Kevin asked us to go to the movies with him and—oops." Christina put her hand to her mouth. "Sorry, I didn't mean to say anything. I mean, it sounds like I'm rubbing it in about Kevin and Lindsay."

"Don't worry about it." Melanie went over to the table to clear the rest of the dishes. "Lindsay and Kevin make a great couple. As long as Kevin's my friend, I'm happy."

"Really?" Christina didn't sound convinced.

"Really. So why aren't you going out with Parker?" Melanie carried the stack of dirty plates to the counter and started scraping the leftover food into the trash.

"He's studying, believe it or not. He's got a calculus test Monday. Actually, he's coming over tonight, too, so I can quiz him on his problems. Hey, why don't you read lines with Katie when she comes? At least until I'm done helping Parker."

"Why doesn't Katie practice with Tony the dreamboat? It won't be nearly as romantic when she and I sing, 'Those summer nigh-*ights!*'" Melanie belted out a few lines of the popular song.

Christina giggled. "I don't know. You're making *me* swoon. So will you help her? She should be here in about forty-five minutes."

"Sure." After they finished cleaning up, Melanie headed upstairs to shower. Christina bounded up the steps right behind Melanie and followed her into the room.

"Belmont is going to be so cool," she exclaimed for the tenth time, throwing herself on Melanie's quilt-covered bed. "I just wish you were riding, too." She sat bolt upright. "I know! Let's convince Ian and Sam to enter Wind Chaser! He's ready."

Pulling out a drawer, Melanie found a clean T-shirt. "No, they've laid up Chaser this month because of his wind puffs, remember?"

"Then how about Fast Gun? Ms. McFarland's got him back in training since he was gelded."

"Just light training. Ian says he needs about three more weeks to be really fit."

"Oh." Christina slumped back on the bed.

Melanie laughed at her cousin's gloomy expression. "Quit worrying. I don't want to ride at Belmont. The pressure would give me a headache, and I'd never get to visit with my folks." She grinned at Christina. "You'll have to make Whitebrook famous all by yourself."

"Gee, thanks," Christina muttered. "Put the pressure on me, why don't you."

"Besides, I want to concentrate on Image. In fact, I may not even go to New York"

Christina feigned shock. "And miss watching *me* ride?" she asked in a princessy voice.

"It's not that I don't want to go," Melanie admitted. "But Image and I had a big setback today, and I don't think I should leave her just now."

"A big setback? What does that mean?"

Melanie should have known her cousin would ask. "It means that when I put the saddle on Image, she blew up, jumped out of the pasture, crashed Fredericka's tea party, and almost ran into the road."

Christina laughed. "Right. Now what *really* happened?"

"That *is* what really happened," Melanie said. Then she filled her cousin in on all the details. When she got to the part about Image running through the party, Melanie jogged around her bedroom, waving her arms and screaming like the ladies at the party. "They went berserk!"

Christina burst out laughing. "I wish I could have been there!"

"That part was kind of funny," Melanie admitted. "But when Image charged down the drive—" She shuddered.

"And Kevin's going to help you, huh?" Christina wiggled her brows.

"Would you *stop*? Kevin and I are friends. Besides, he wants to see Image have a chance on the track, too."

"Whatever you say." The doorbell rang, and Christina gasped. "That must be Parker, and I haven't even brushed my teeth!" She jumped off the bed. "I can't wait to tell him about Gratis," she said, and with an excited squeal, she ran from the room.

Melanie exhaled loudly. Christina was as high as a kite. And she should be. Everything was going her way.

Jealous? Melanie asked herself. She shook her head, then caught herself. *All right, just a little.*

Grabbing her clean clothes, Melanie headed to the bathroom. *Get over it, Graham,* she told herself. She was doing what she wanted—working with Image.

Maybe it was going to be harder than Melanie had first thought. But with Kevin's help, she was up for the challenge. When Image won her first race, it would be because of Melanie and Kevin's hard work, dedication, and faith in Image.

She'd have no one to be jealous of then. And some people might even be a teeny bit jealous of *her*.

"Go, Kevin, Go!" Melanie, Lindsay, and Beth McLean cheered. It was Thursday afternoon, and Melanie had stayed after school to watch Henry Clay's varsity soccer game against Fordham High. The week had flown by, filled with schoolwork, driving practice, and working with Image. On Sunday Kevin had gone with Melanie to meet Image and Fredericka. Melanie was delighted to see that they both liked him. The rest of the week Melanie had groomed Image and then worked on ground manners.

Image had behaved so perfectly, Melanie sometimes wondered if Saturday's escapade had been only a dream.

"Drive it in, Kevin!" Kevin's mom shouted. Beth never missed any of her son's games. She knew every player on every team and all the rules. Lindsay was on the girls' soccer team, and through the whole game she and Beth had heatedly discussed every move.

Melanie was too embarrassed to admit she knew nothing about soccer, but she did know that when Kevin kicked the ball past the goalie and into the net, he'd scored another goal for the Henry Clay Cougars. Jumping up, she cheered loudly.

Lindsay grabbed her by the shoulders. "Kevin scored the winning goal!" she screeched, her ponytail swinging wildly as she hopped up and down. "We won!"

"The game's over already?" Melanie asked, but Lindsay had already turned toward Beth, and the loud cheering drowned out Melanie's question. Out on the field, Kevin was mobbed by his teammates. Glancing toward the bleachers, he raised his arm and gave them a thumbs-up sign. Lindsay blew him a kiss, and Beth yelled, "That's the way, honey!" Melanie grinned, glad she'd decided to come.

Breaking away from his teammates, Kevin jogged over. "Mom, a scout from the University of Kentucky was watching the game," he said excitedly.

"Oh, Kevin!" Beth gave him a hug, immediately

pulling back with a grimace. "Yuck. You are *really* sweaty."

"Yeah." Still grinning, his gaze went from Lindsay to Melanie, then back to his mom. "Thanks for coming, guys. Well, I'd better get showered."

"I'll wait for you, Kevin," Lindsay said.

"Melanie? You want a ride with me?" Beth asked. Melanie nodded. She had managed to get through the game without feeling too strange about sitting next to Kevin's new girlfriend, but there was no way she wanted to ride with them in Kevin's truck. "Could you drop me off at Tall Oaks?" she asked Beth. "I want to work with Image before it gets too dark."

"Sure." On the way Beth chattered excitedly about Kevin's chances for a scholarship. Melanie liked Kevin's mom. She was down-to-earth, and though she wasn't involved with the farm, she was very active, teaching aerobics at the nearby YMCA and writing fitness articles for magazines.

When they arrived at Tall Oaks, Melanie noticed an unfamiliar truck parked by the barn. Hopping from the car, she made sure that Elizabeth could give her a ride home before saying good-bye to Beth.

The sun was setting, and Melanie knew she didn't have much time with Image. Grabbing a grooming bucket and lead line, she hurried through the barn. She heard voices coming from Khan's stall but didn't stop to find out who it was.

When she jogged down the hill, Image greeted her

with a welcoming nicker. "Hey, my black beauty," Melanie crooned as she went through the gate.

Dropping the bucket, she hooked the lead on the halter. Image snuffled her jean pockets, hunting for treats. Melanie fed her a carrot, then started brushing her dusty coat. She talked as she brushed, quietly explaining to Image how exciting races were. "You burst out of the starting gate as if you were on fire. Then you gallop around the track toward the finish line. The object is to run faster than all the other horses and cross the line first." She pointed the brush at Image. "And I can tell you're the kind of horse who will *hate* losing."

Image bobbed her head as if in agreement. Moving toward the filly's flank, Melanie began to brush out her thick tail. Suddenly Image stepped backward, ripping the long black strands from her fingers.

"Whoa!" Melanie said in a firm voice.

Image had thrown her head high and was staring intently at the barn. "What is it, girl?"

Melanie moved toward the fence to get a better look. Two people were standing in the shadows of the doorway, watching them.

Melanie stared, trying to figure out who they were, but they turned and disappeared into the barn. Shrugging, she finished grooming Image. By then it was dark. She picked up the filly's feet, making her stand quietly while she cleaned each one, then decided to quit.

"On Saturday Kevin's coming to help," she told the filly. "We're going to longe you, which I'm sure you'll hate," she added under her breath. "But by then the round pen should be finished." She stroked Image's forehead. "And even if you run away, there will be no place for you to go, except in a circle."

With a last kiss good-bye, Melanie headed to the barn. The inside lights were on, bathing the stalls in a yellow glow. Melanie put away her supplies, then tracked down Elizabeth, who was turning out a horse for the night.

"Need help?" Melanie asked.

"Yeah. When Mr. Townsend showed up, I had to drop everything. It put me behind."

"Brad was here?" Melanie asked.

"Yup. Left about ten minutes ago." Elizabeth handed Melanie a lead rope. "You can turn Charles out with Danger. Then I'll be done."

"Why was he here?" Melanie followed Elizabeth down the aisle.

She shrugged. "Looking at horses, I guess. Later he and Alexis were talking for a long time, but I was too busy mucking out stalls to eavesdrop. Then they left together."

"I didn't know Alexis was buddies with Brad," Melanie said. Then she remembered that Brad was the one who had recommended Alexis to Fredericka.

"Ha ha." Elizabeth gave an exaggerated laugh. "Alexis makes sure she's buddies with everybody

119

who's rich and powerful. Isn't that how you get ahead in the Thoroughbred business?" She made a face. "Mucking out stalls obviously isn't the way."

"I guess." Melanie went to get Charles, who was banging on his stall door, eager to go out and play. "Hold your horses," she told him.

As she led the colt outside she wondered what Brad and Alexis had been discussing. Did it have anything to do with Image? At the Freedmans' party Brad had acted awfully interested in the filly.

No, don't be silly, Melanie told herself. Then she remembered what Kevin had said about Brad wanting to buy Townsend Mistress, Image's dam, but the Grabers wouldn't sell her. Was Brad interested in Image now?

When Melanie let Charles loose, goose bumps prickled up and down her arms. And it wasn't because of the cool night air.

11

"CHRISTINA, YOU'LL RIDE DAZZLE IN A RACE FOR FILLIES and Rhapsody in an allowance race." Ashleigh was reading off the roster. It was Friday after the morning workouts, and the girls were in the barn office going over their jockey assignments for Saturday's races.

"I'm also riding Dark Wind for June, and Sunny Gold for Mr. Crizer," Christina said.

"Hold on. Let's make sure none of those races conflict," Ashleigh said, writing something down. "Now, Melanie, I've got you on Raven in a maiden race and Pride in the Turfway II Allowance."

Looking over Ashleigh's shoulder, Melanie checked the racing program. "Pride's in the last race. Can Naomi Traeger ride him instead? I was hoping to finish in time to work with Image."

"Well, okay." Ashleigh looked surprised. "But that's only one race for you."

Melanie shrugged, and Ashleigh looked at Christina as if hoping for an explanation. "She's into being a trainer now, Mom," Christina said.

"Oh. How's it going with Image, anyway?" Ashleigh asked.

"Great!" Melanie's eyes lit up. "Image is behaving perfectly when I groom and lead her."

"What else are you doing with her?"

"Uh, nothing." Melanie's excitement faded. "I know it doesn't sound like a lot."

"But it is!" Christina chimed in. "She was practically wild before Melanie started working with her."

"Then I guess that is good progress," Ashleigh said, but Melanie could tell her aunt wasn't too impressed. Which was understandable. Image was a two-year-old—she should have started racing already.

"Chris, what race are you riding Honor in?" Ashleigh said, beckoning her daughter closer as she bent over the training books. "I want to make sure there are no conflicts."

Melanie left them to it and jogged up to the house. Every morning there was a rush to get ready for school, and she and Christina had to hustle to get there for their first class at ten-thirty. Melanie thought about going back and telling Ashleigh she didn't want to race at all this weekend. But then she decided against it. She had to keep racing, otherwise she'd be a bug forever.

And she needed to keep honing her skills so she'd be ready to ride Image when the filly was finally ready.

A slow smile spread across Melanie's face when she thought about Image's first race. She couldn't wait.

Raven was a dainty black two-year-old. Melanie watched the filly mince around the saddling paddock. It was Saturday, and Melanie was riding Raven in Turfway's first race of the day. The filly was full of herself, and Maureen Mack, Whitebrook's assistant trainer, had to keep a firm hold on the lead.

As Melanie watched, she couldn't help but compare Raven to Image. Both two-year-olds had glossy black coats and pretty dished faces. But Raven was slender and streamlined, while Image was built more like a colt, with well-defined muscles, a deep girth, and powerful shoulders. As Melanie compared the fillies, a rush of excitement filled her. Physically, Image outpowered them all.

Maureen led Raven into the saddling stall and threw the number-five blanket across her back. Melanie set her racing saddle on top of the blanket and helped Maureen make sure it was in just the right place. When Maureen tightened the girth, Raven pinned her ears and squealed.

Maureen rolled her eyes. "She's going to be a handful," she told Melanie. "We upped her ration of protein this past week, so beware."

Melanie listened closely. Maureen had been Ian's assistant for several years, and she knew all the Whitebrook horses well. Melanie had gotten into trouble in a race on Fast Gun because she'd been too cocky to heed Maureen's advice. She wouldn't make that mistake again.

"Keep her away from the pack as much as possible," Maureen went on, "even if it means going wide. And keep her focused on you. She's really acting mareish—kicking out at the other fillies."

Melanie patted Raven's shoulder. "We'll do fine, right, pretty girl?"

Maureen led Raven from the stall and paraded her around the oval.

"Riders up!" the paddock judge shouted.

Melanie adjusted her helmet strap as she hurried over. Maureen gave her a leg up and led her to the gate. Raven jigged down the track past the grandstand. The crowd in the stands was lighter than it had been for Labor Day weekend, but there were still a lot of fans.

Christina was riding several horses later, but Melanie wouldn't be staying to watch. Kevin was picking her up at three o'clock so that they could drive back to Lexington, get a bite to eat, and then head over to Tall Oaks to work with Image.

As they neared the starting gate Melanie urged Raven into a quiet canter. The number-six horse came up beside them, and Raven swished her tail in warning.

"Behave," Melanie scolded her, giving her a light smack on the neck. "Concentrate on the race and quit worrying about who's on your butt."

While the other horses were being loaded into the gate, Melanie checked out the competition. The two horses she had to watch were Silk 'n' Lace, a gray filly, and Petite Four, a bay. Both were ridden by top jockeys. She spotted Fred on a chestnut called Windy Day, but he posed little threat. Since he'd become a bug, Fred hadn't won a race. Not that he was a bad rider—he just hadn't gotten good mounts.

Catching Fred's eye, Melanie waved and mouthed, "Good luck." Fred waggled his stick at her. Melanie hadn't seen or talked to him since the concert two weeks before.

When it came time for Raven to be led into the starting gate, the filly rolled her eyes and balked. The assistant starter tugged on the bridle. "Come on now, missy," he said gruffly. "Be good."

Melanie groaned. All the Whitebrook horses were carefully and patiently trained to walk into the narrow gates. She didn't know why Raven was being so cranky, but it was kind of embarrassing.

"Sorry. She's being a real witch today," she apologized to the handler.

"I know. The blue-and-white horses usually go in nicely," he said, referring to Whitebrook's colors. "I'll try to sweet-talk her in."

But a minute later, when Raven wouldn't budge,

two other starters linked hands behind her rump and, whistling and shouting, shoved her in. The door slammed shut, and Melanie took a breath. Loading problems happened to every jockey, she knew, but it always held things up and made the other horses and jockeys testy.

Finally the number-seven horse was loaded. By then Raven was pulsing with contained energy. Her ears were pricked, and she danced on her forelegs. Melanie hoped she could keep the filly's attention focused on the race ahead.

"It's post time!" the announcer called across the track.

Melanie readied herself. Thoughts of Image entered her head, but she pushed them away. She couldn't make the same mistake she had two weeks earlier. This was her only race of the day, and she had to make it a good one.

The starter's gun went off. Raven burst from the starting gate, galloped hard two strides, then suddenly stumbled.

Melanie fell onto the filly's neck. Grasping the short mane, she clung tightly, trying not to unbalance Raven further as the filly desperately tried to untangle her legs. By the time her stride was even, the field was several lengths ahead.

Melanie gritted her teeth. It was a short race, and Raven wasn't a come-from-behind horse. Plus the filly hated the dirt clods hitting her face and the dust clogging her nostrils. Melanie's only choice was to steer wide.

Melanie flexed her fingers on the right rein while pumping hard with her body. Raven stretched out her nose and galloped with all her heart. Melanie kept low. She didn't even tilt her head to check the distance poles. She could tell by the curve of the track, the horses they passed, and the seconds ticking off in her brain how far they'd raced and how far they had to go.

Ahead she saw the rear end of the gray, Silk 'n' Lace, who was also on the outside. The jockey had her rated, which meant the filly had energy to spare. Melanie urged Raven on, closing the gap between them.

They galloped neck and neck. Cocking her head to the left, Melanie checked out the rest of the field. Raven and Silk 'n' Lace were in the lead. The horses on the inside had fallen slightly back. As they rounded the turn to the finish line, Melanie could hear Raven's labored breathing. The stumble coupled with the mad dash to catch up had cost the filly dearly.

"Give it all you've got," Melanie whispered, but she knew in her heart that Raven had already given it her all. The gray surged ahead. Out of the corner of her eye, Melanie saw Windy Day coming up fast on the rail, followed by Petite Four. The chestnut passed Raven on the inside, blew past Silk 'n' Lace, and crossed the finish line first.

When they galloped past the finish pole, Melanie

stood in her stirrups, slowing Raven. The filly's breath came in ragged bursts.

"Easy, girl," Melanie crooned. Ahead of them, Fred was punching his fist in the air, a triumphant expression on his face. Melanie flashed him a smile. It was Fred's first win, and she knew he'd never forget it.

When Raven dropped down to a walk, Melanie quickly dismounted and pulled the reins over the filly's head. Raven's nostrils were flared, and her neck glistened with sweat. Maureen jogged onto the track. "Is she okay?"

"I think so," Melanie said, trying to catch her own breath. "Really blowing, though. She tried so hard. I hope Ashleigh and Mike won't be disappointed."

Maureen shook her head. Snapping the lead to Raven's bridle, she fell into stride next to Melanie, keeping the filly moving. "We just haven't found her niche. What happened coming out of the gate?"

"She broke great, then almost fell. I have no idea why."

Halting Raven, Maureen stooped and ran her hand down her front legs. "Looks like she clipped her front right heel. Wasn't anyone's fault."

After unbuckling the girth, Melanie pulled off the saddle. When Maureen led the filly off, Melanie watched them go. Even though it wasn't her fault, she'd blown her only race of the day. She checked the tote board. They'd come in fourth out of seven.

At least Fred had won. Since she didn't have any more races, Melanie decided to go see him in the winner's circle. Mounted on Windy Day, he was beaming for the photographer. Melanie recognized the older man standing by Windy's head, holding the trophy along with a woman in a fancy dress. It was Jimmy J, the trainer Fred had been talking to at Monty Freedman's party.

"Wow, that felt great," Fred said later when Melanie walked with him back to the jockey room. His face was flushed, and his eyes glowed.

"You deserve it," Melanie said, pleased for her friend.

"Now that Jimmy J's taken me under his wing, maybe I'll be winning a little more often."

"That's great!" Melanie said.

They reached the jockey room. As soon as they went inside George yelled, "Hey, Graham, your race is being replayed. Better hurry if you wanna catch your big stumble."

Ignoring George's smirk, Melanie moved closer to the TV. On the screen, Raven broke cleanly from the gate, strode strongly forward, and then took an abrupt nosedive.

"What's wrong, Mel, losing your winning touch?" George nudged Sammy Fingers, who sat next to him.

Striding around the sofa, Fred stopped in front of the older jockey. "Hey, George, don't you have anything better to do than flap your big mouth?"

"Ooh. Anderson finally wins one race and thinks he's a hotshot."

"Come on, Fred," Melanie said, pulling him away. "Since George has been on a losing streak, he has a big chip on his shoulder. A *cow* chip," Melanie added, and Sammy Fingers burst out laughing.

George scowled. "At least I'm riding, Graham. I haven't noticed too many trainers asking for you."

Melanie shrugged, determined not to let George get to her. "Been too busy."

"Doing what? Crashing parties? I heard that after your boyfriend dumped you, you were so hard up you had to take a horse to Fredericka Graber's tea party."

Melanie's cheeks reddened. She had been wondering when someone would bring up Image's escapade. "You know, George, someday I'm going to get tired of your big mouth."

George only chuckled. "You think I'm scared of someone too wimpy to lead a horse? I heard that Vince is only letting you work with that filly so he can get a good laugh."

Melanie's fingers curled into fists. "Well, the laugh's going to be on you when that filly and I start winning races."

For a second George didn't say a word. Then he threw back his head and burst out laughing. "That's the funniest thing I ever heard. I guess the question is, will you be riding her over the finish line, or will she be dragging you?"

Melanie's eyes narrowed into slits. She would have loved to punch George right in the face. Instead she whirled around and ran into the women's locker room, George's laughter trailing after her.

The door shut behind her. Melanie looked down, realizing her hands were still balled into fists. Why had she let George get to her? She'd taken worse ribbings than that. Plopping on the bench in front of her locker, she put her head in her hands.

She knew why she'd gotten so mad: George had touched a raw nerve. Several raw nerves, in fact. Her boyfriend *had* dumped her, she *had* lost her winning touch, and it was true that no trainers were beating down her door.

With a sigh, Melanie opened her locker and pulled out clean clothes. Obviously she and Image were the biggest joke around the track. But all that meant was that she'd have to work even harder and show them all.

12

"I'VE GOT TO FIGURE OUT WHAT WILL WORK BEST WITH Image," Melanie said as she and Kevin drove to Tall Oaks.

Sitting sideways, she tucked one leg under the other. She ran her fingers through her still shower-damp hair, bit her lower lip, and then began to jiggle her foot. "What do you think?" she asked Kevin. "Should I get tougher with her? Try more psychology? A chain over her nose?"

"I think," Kevin said, "that you should relax."

"Relax! How can I? Any minute Vince Jones will show up at Fredericka's, point his finger at me, and say, 'You had your chance, and you failed.'"

"Has Fredericka given up yet?"

"No."

"Then what are you worrying about? She's the owner. You can't let jerks like George get to you."

"I know." Melanie shifted and faced front. Exhaling loudly, she slid down until her head was resting on the back of the seat. "The problem is that I'm really worried I'm going to fail, Kevin."

"Hey, do you know why I'm one of the best soccer players on the team?" Kevin asked, his eyes on the road as they turned into Fredericka's drive.

"Because you're fast and you love to hit balls with your head and—"

"No. Because I practice more than anyone else, I work hard, and I never give up. Even when we're losing."

He parked the pickup truck by the barn next to Fredericka's huge horse van. Then he turned to face Melanie. "How hard are you willing to work with Image?"

"I'm willing to work *really* hard," Melanie declared. "But what if I fail?"

"Don't think like that. Take the word *fail* out of your vocabulary," Kevin said, opening the truck door. "Anyway, today we are going to tame Her Highness, and all your worrying will have been for nothing."

"Yeah, right," Melanie said, and followed Kevin into the barn.

Alexis was grooming Khan in crossties. The stallion arched his neck, trumpeted at the two strangers, then struck out with one hoof. Alexis tugged sharply on his halter. "Stand," she said firmly. "We don't need *two* brats in this barn."

Melanie wasn't sure if she was trying to be funny or mean. She introduced Kevin, then asked, "Is it all right if we use the round pen?"

"Sure." For a second Alexis scrutinized Kevin, then turned back to Melanie. "Elizabeth is using it to work one of the weanlings, but she should be finished any minute. Nice meeting you, Kevin. And good luck with Image."

Melanie stopped by the tack room. "She seems nice," Kevin said when they were out of earshot.

"Oh, she is—whenever she wants to be." Melanie picked up a lead line, protective leg wraps, and the coiled longe line. "I think she's pretty ambitious. Sometimes I wonder why she stays at Tall Oaks. It's pretty small compared to farms like Townsend Acres."

"Maybe she likes Fredericka."

Melanie snorted. "I doubt that's the reason. She's probably just waiting for a better offer." She handed Kevin the longe line and leg wraps. "I'll go get Image and meet you at the round pen. I want to practice leading her from her pasture."

The round pen had been built in the pasture adjoining Image's. It was in the middle of the field next to the parking area, which also had been fenced off. Fredericka had designed it so that if a horse got loose, it couldn't get to the road.

Image seemed glad to see Melanie, greeting her with a whicker of delight. Melanie snapped the lead to the halter and opened the gate.

"No brushing today," she explained. "We have something even more fun to do. An adventure." She made her voice as calm as possible, though inside she was a bundle of nerves. This was the first time she'd done anything new with Image since the filly had jumped out of the pasture.

She led Image through the gate, closing it behind her. Image nickered nervously to Pedro. Kevin had opened the gate to the round pen, which was made of heavy oak boards and thick posts. It was small enough to work babies, but large enough for a full-grown horse to canter around it in a tight circle.

When Melanie led her into the pen, Image's ears flicked nervously. The walls of the pen were eight feet high, there were no corners, and it was filled with a soft footing. There was no way Image could hurt herself.

Melanie walked the filly around, switched directions, and made her halt. After she and Kevin put the wraps on her, she unsnapped the lead line so that the filly could explore. Throwing up her head, Image trotted back and forth, calling to Pedro. When he didn't answer, she settled down and finally walked up to Melanie for a treat.

"Good girl." Melanie patted her neck. "You want to try working with her?" she asked Kevin, who was watching by the gate. They had planned to longe Image briefly if she was quiet. Kevin had taught hundreds of yearlings to longe, and Melanie wanted to see how he started them.

"Sure." He patted his pocket. "I came prepared with my own treats."

"When I lead her, I've worked on voice commands," she told Kevin. "Walk, trot, halt. You could try them when you're longing."

Kevin came in and ran his hand down the filly's chest. Melanie felt her earlier anxiety fade. She'd forgotten how calm and confident Kevin was around horses.

"The key is to start with the horse close to you, so you can keep control," Kevin said as he snapped the longe line to her halter. "Feed out a little line, and step away from the horse's shoulder slightly toward the flank. You don't want to get ahead of her as she circles you."

He demonstrated. "Walk," he crooned, and Image moved out. When she tried to stop and turn his way, he got slightly behind her, clucked, and waved the coil of rope to push her forward.

Melanie held her breath, waiting for Image to blow up, kick out, or do something else horrible, but the filly moved in a circle as smoothly as a carousel horse.

"One hand controls the line to the head while the other uses the coil to move her forward," Kevin explained. "Never let the line wrap around your hand. You don't want to get dragged."

Waving the coil of rope, Kevin told the filly to trot. Image broke into a smooth trot.

Melanie smiled. The filly's gaits were so fluid, so

strong. It was like watching a dream. When Image had walked and trotted in both directions, Kevin called out firmly, "Halt," and the filly stopped squarely.

Melanie applauded. "She was perfect for you! Let's stop while she's being such an angel. You can teach me how to longe her tomorrow."

"Okay." Kevin scratched Image under the forelock, then led her toward the gate. Melanie swung it open and stepped back.

"She was *too* good for you," Melanie said. "I almost wish she'd try something bad so you could show me what to do."

"The secret is always to pay attention," Kevin said, leading Image through the opening. "And keep one step—"

A truck motor roared to life, drowning out the rest of his words. Someone had started Fredericka's horse van, which was parked by the front of the barn. Suddenly the truck backfired, the noise as sharp and loud as the blast of a rifle.

Image jumped straight in the air and twisted sideways. When she landed, her left shoulder slammed into Kevin, knocking him into the gatepost. The truck backfired again, and Image leaped forward, but Kevin had locked his hands on the rope and swung her around with all his might. White-eyed, Image came to a jerky stop in front of him. She was trembling all over.

"Easy, girl!" Melanie hurried over. Taking hold of

the cheekpiece of Image's halter, she soothed the frightened filly. With another sharp report, the truck rumbled down the drive.

"You're okay. It's not going to hurt you," Melanie crooned. Her heart banged as she waited for Image to rear or tear away. But the filly only danced in place. When the truck drove out of sight, Melanie relaxed her grip on the halter.

"Thanks for hanging on to her, Kevin." Melanie turned back toward the pen. Kevin was bent over, holding his right knee with both hands. "What happened? Are you okay?"

He shook his head. "No. I whacked the outside of my knee on the gatepost. It's killing me."

"I'll put Image away, then come back and help you." Clucking, she trotted Image to her pasture and turned her out with Pedro. Instead of charging off to see her buddy, Image looked at Melanie with a puzzled expression in her huge eyes.

Melanie gave her one last pat, then rushed to the round pen. Kevin was leaning against the gatepost, his face ashen. "It hurts too much to put weight on it. You're going to have to help me back to my truck."

He draped his arm around Melanie's shoulders. Using her as a crutch, he hopped to the gate that opened into the parking lot. Elizabeth hurried out of the barn. "What happened?"

Kevin tried to smile, but Melanie could tell it was forced. "I forgot to listen to my own advice."

Elizabeth opened the gate, alarm filling her eyes. "Did Image kick you?"

"No. She ran into me," Kevin said as he hopped through. "She freaked out when that truck backfired."

Elizabeth glanced toward the spot where the van had been parked. "Alexis was driving it. She knows that old thing backfires like a cannon. She should have warned you."

"Maybe she didn't know we were in the round pen yet." Melanie glanced at Kevin, then at Elizabeth. "We've got to get his knee looked at. This is a soccer star here. Nothing can happen to him."

"Lexington General's close by."

"I don't think Kevin can drive."

"I'll drive," Elizabeth volunteered. "I've got my mom's car today."

Kevin hopped across the parking area to Elizabeth's car. Holding his knee, he slid into the front seat. "Ouch, that hurt."

Melanie climbed into the backseat, her heart heavy. Kevin's knee had to be all right or she'd never forgive herself.

"It's a hematoma," Dr. Matthews, the emergency-room doctor, said two hours later

By that time Beth had arrived, Elizabeth had gone back to Tall Oaks, Kevin's knee had been X-rayed, and Melanie had leafed through twenty magazines.

"That sounds terrible," Beth breathed.

"It's another term for a bad bruise," Dr. Matthews explained.

"Well, at least nothing's broken," Kevin said. He was sitting on the edge of the table in the examination room. Melanie was leaning against a wall, trying to make herself invisible. Beth stood by her son, holding his hand.

"Kevin told me he plays soccer for Henry Clay High," Dr. Matthews said to Beth. "Unfortunately, a hematoma's going to sideline him for at least three weeks."

Melanie cringed. She glanced at Kevin. All the blood had drained from his face, but he didn't say anything. In fact, since they'd left Tall Oaks, he'd barely said two words.

"I'm going to wrap it, Kevin," Dr. Matthews continued as she got out an Ace bandage. "You'll need to stay off your leg for a day or two, keep it elevated, and keep an ice pack on your knee until the swelling goes down. And absolutely no soccer until there's no pain."

Out of the corner of her eye, Melanie saw Beth give Kevin an anguished look. Melanie wanted to cry. She knew how important soccer was to Kevin and how crucial this season was. If he couldn't play, he might not get that college scholarship.

All because of Image.

Melanie had to confront the truth. Vince Jones was right—Image was nothing but bad luck.

13

"BETH, KEVIN, I'M SO SORRY," MELANIE APOLOGIZED FOR the tenth time when Beth stopped in front of the Reeses' farmhouse to let her off.

Kevin stared out the window with a stony expression. Beth glanced over her shoulder at Melanie, but her smile wasn't very forgiving. "It wasn't your fault, Melanie."

But Melanie knew it was. She knew Image was crazy and unpredictable, yet she'd still begged Kevin to help her.

"If there's anything I can do . . ." Her voice trailed off, because she knew there wasn't. Kevin wouldn't be able to play soccer for weeks. He might lose his chance at a scholarship. He'd probably never talk to her again. How could she ever repair that much damage?

Opening the car door, she slid out. Kevin still hadn't said anything. She shut the door and slowly

141

walked around to the entrance that led into the mud room. She unlaced her sneakers, letting them fall to the floor with a bang. Then she went into the kitchen.

Ashleigh was alone at the table, sipping a cup of hot tea and eating a slice of apple pie. "Hi! How's Kevin's knee?" Setting down her mug, Ashleigh frowned expectantly at Melanie.

Melanie dropped wearily into the chair. "It's a hematoma," she said, and explained everything. By the time she got to the part about Kevin not playing soccer, tears were rolling down her cheeks. Reaching over, Ashleigh put her hand on Melanie's shoulder.

"I'm so sorry, Mel," Ashleigh said, handing her a napkin. "But quit blaming yourself. Any young horse might have reacted the same way Image did to the van backfiring."

"But Image keeps messing up. She got Chris and Gratis hurt, she dragged me all over the place, she got loose at Fredericka's party, and now Kevin." Melanie ticked them off on her fingers. "She's bad luck, and I've decided she's not worth it."

"Not worth it?" Ashleigh cocked one brow. "Are you sure? The way you talk about her, she sounds pretty special."

"She is, Aunt Ashleigh, but I can't risk it. I mean, who will she hurt next? I might as well face it—I'm not a trainer. Now Vince, Brad, and George and all the others who have been laughing at me can stop laughing. I'm through."

Ashleigh didn't say anything. *That's because she knows I'm right*, Melanie thought, wiping the tears from her cheeks with another napkin.

"I saved you some dinner and a piece of pie," Ashleigh said. "Want to eat now?"

"I guess I am kind of hungry. Where's everyone else?"

"Christina went to Whisperwood with Parker. He's working on a difficult dressage test with Foxy, and he wanted Chris to watch him. Mike and Ian went over to Vince Jones's to make arrangements for Star to be shipped to Belmont. He's leaving a week from Tuesday."

Ashleigh fixed a plate of fried chicken, green beans, and one of Beth's homemade rolls, and set it down in front of Melanie. Her mouth began to water. She hadn't realized how hungry she was.

"Melanie." Ashleigh sat back down in the chair. "I'm sorry that Kevin got hurt. But if you believe in Image, then you can't give up on her. Remember all the problems I had with Wonder? No one except me thought she would amount to anything. And that's all it took—one person with a dream and a lot of hard work."

"That's because you knew in your heart that Wonder would one day be a champion," Melanie said dejectedly. "I've finally realized that Image really doesn't have what it takes. She's too stubborn and unpredictable and—"

143

Ashleigh gave Melanie such a long, hard stare that she cut her sentence short. "Is that the only reason you've been working with Image, Melanie?" Ashleigh asked. "Because you want to prove to the world that she'll be a winner? If it is, then it *won't* work."

Melanie caught her breath. Was Ashleigh right? Had she only been using Image to prove something to herself and everybody else? If she had, then she'd lost sight of what had first drawn her to the filly—that Image was a horse she could fall in love with. Or rather, that she did indeed love.

Melanie blinked back her tears. "But what about Kevin? He's never going to forgive me."

"What's that about me?"

Melanie spun in her chair. Kevin stood in the doorway of the mud room, leaning on his crutches. Dropping her fork, Melanie jumped up. "I didn't hear you come in. How'd you get here? What are you doing here?"

"I hobbled over from the house." He waved one crutch in the air. "I know I look pathetic, but I figured I'd better get used to these things."

"But Dr. Matthews said to keep your leg elevated," Melanie reminded him.

"Here, sit down, Kevin." Ashleigh pulled out a chair. Kevin swung over and plopped into it. Melanie took the crutches while Ashleigh pulled up another chair for Kevin to prop his foot on.

"How about some chicken?" Ashleigh asked, fixing him a plate before he could even reply. When she set it in front of Kevin, he attacked the chicken and then started on the green beans.

Melanie picked at her own food. For a second Ashleigh watched them eat, then she said, "I think I'll take my tea and go out to the barn office. There's some work I need to finish."

"Why don't you do it here?" Melanie suggested quickly. She wasn't sure why Kevin had come to the house, but if he was still mad, she didn't want to be alone with him.

"No. You two need to talk."

Thanks, Aunt Ashleigh, Melanie grumbled miserably to herself. When Ashleigh left, Melanie's gaze dropped to her plate.

Kevin chuckled. "Don't worry, I'm not going to bite your head off. In fact, I want to apologize for being such a jerk."

"I deserved it," Melanie said.

"No, you didn't. I was just trying to find someone to blame. Someone to be mad at." He shrugged. "I don't know how this will affect my soccer scholarship. But I do know it will blow the season for me. By the time my knee heals and I get in shape again, most of the games will be over."

"You have every right to be furious," Melanie said. "A soccer scholarship and a championship trophy your senior year—those were your dreams."

"I know. But when I cooled off, I realized it was no one's fault. Not yours or mine or Image's."

145

"We could blame Alexis for starting that stupid van," Melanie said, a giggle of relief rising in her throat now that she knew Kevin wouldn't be mad at her forever.

"But I am sorry," she apologized again. "If I were you, I wouldn't forgive me or Image. Image thinks she can do whatever she wants to whomever she wants to do it to."

"The other thing I wanted to tell you is that you shouldn't give up on Image." Kevin pointed his fork at her. "I know that's what you and Ashleigh were talking about. Image is *your* dream. Just because mine turned into a disaster doesn't mean yours has to."

"Ashleigh said the same thing. And what she told me reminded me that I fell in love with Image right away, though it's hard to understand what I see in that pigheaded filly." Melanie propped her elbows on the table and leaned forward. "But I still don't know what to do with Image. You were my last hope. And look what happened." She gestured toward his leg.

"There has to be something else we can do." He tapped the spoon on the table, his gaze drifting to the kitchen counter. "I sure could think better if I was eating apple pie."

Laughing, Melanie brought over what was left in the pie plate. "I get the hint. You can have my piece."

"Are you sure?" Kevin asked, but he was already digging in.

"I need someone to help me," Melanie said, sitting back down. "Your dad and Mike are too busy,

Christina's getting Star in shape for Belmont, Parker's got Foxy to worry about, and Ashleigh ... do you think she'd help?" Melanie brightened, then remembered that Ashleigh was trying to get everything done around the farm before they left for New York the next week.

"Everybody I trust is too busy," Melanie said with a sigh, her hopes fading. "And I just can't do it alone. Image needs someone who demands her respect and won't give her treats just for putting her ears forward, like I do. She needs—" Suddenly it dawned on her. *"Pirate!"*

"Pirate?" Kevin repeated, the last forkful of pie poised in front of his mouth.

"Yes!" Melanie's eyes widened with excitement. "I should have thought of him in the first place. Who better to teach Image to be humble and submissive?"

Kevin looked doubtful. "I don't know. Pirate's put a lot of rambunctious yearlings in their places, but a grown filly?"

"I think it will work. Since he's been blind, Pirate's learned to take care of himself. He doesn't let anyone boss him, but he's not mean about it. He'd be perfect!"

"It's worth a try. But you have to convince Fredericka. She may not want some big gelding bossing around her princess."

Jumping up, Melanie headed for the telephone. "You're right. I'll just have to tell Fredericka that Pirate might be Image's last chance."

And it may be my *last chance*, Melanie thought, *to show Image that I love her too much to give up.*

Sunday, when Melanie unloaded Pirate from the Whitebrook horse trailer, Alexis stood in the barn doorway, her hands on her hips. Joe Kisner, who had driven them over, nodded politely to the Tall Oaks farm manager, but Alexis turned on her heel and disappeared into the barn.

"We're here, Pirate," Melanie said. Raising his head, Pirate smelled the air.

Dani came around the side of the trailer carrying a feed tub. All summer she'd been using Pirate as a pony horse. When she'd found out Pirate was going to Tall Oaks, she'd asked if she could come along to help him get used to the new place.

"You'll only be here for a little while," Dani told him, and Melanie could hear a catch in her voice.

"And Dani will visit you every day," Melanie added, reassuring them both.

Just then Fredericka came up the drive. "Oh, he's a handsome lad!" she exclaimed. "Image will love him. She's needed a better-looking companion than Pedro."

"And Pedro needs a vacation from Image," Melanie said, laughing. The night before, it hadn't taken her long to convince Fredericka that putting Pirate in with Image was a good idea. Not that Melanie could guarantee it would work, but Fredericka had agreed that they didn't have many other choices.

Earlier Image had been put in her stall, and Pedro had been moved to a different paddock to baby-sit a foal that had just been weaned. Melanie wanted Pirate to get used to the pasture before she introduced the two horses.

Dani led him down the hill and through the gate. She walked him slowly around the perimeter, letting him touch the fence with his nose. Then she took him inside the run-in shed. Putting his head down, he blew noisily, taking in the new scents. After about fifteen minutes, Dani unsnapped the lead rope.

Since Pirate had been blind for several years, he'd learned to navigate new territory. As long as there wasn't anything unusual or dangerous to get into, he was adept at finding his way around.

"He's incredible," Fredericka said after they'd watched him for a while. "But do you think he'll be able to take care of himself?"

"Yes, I do," Melanie said.

Head low to the ground, Pirate continued to check out his new quarters. Melanie was glad to see he was more curious than apprehensive. And when he settled down and started grazing, she decided it was time to introduce Image.

As soon as Melanie led Image from the barn, the filly jerked to a halt, her eyes on the strange horse in her pasture. She trumpeted loudly, her tone imperious.

Tossing her neck, she danced all the way down the hill. Melanie held tightly to the lead rope and used her voice and body to keep the filly next to her. But Image was a coiled spring of tension. Melanie suddenly had doubts. What if Image hurt Pirate, too?

"Oh, my," Melanie heard Fredericka murmur as Image pranced to the gate, her tail switching with undisguised irritation. Even Dani looked worried. Joe opened the gate, winking at Melanie. He was the only one who didn't seem concerned. "Don't worry. He'll show her who's boss."

Melanie led Image through the gate, told her to behave, and let her go.

Image cantered over to Pirate, bellowing her anger. *How dare you eat my grass! This is my territory!* she seemed to be saying. Her ears were flat on her head, her tail arched and waving. Melanie gulped. Pirate was taller, heavier, and more muscular than the younger filly, but Image didn't seem to care.

Melanie shut one eye. Fredericka clutched her hand. "Dear me," she whispered. "This isn't going to be pretty."

When Image was almost in front of Pirate, the big gelding lifted his head, swung his hindquarters toward her, and cocked one hoof. Image slid to a halt, a surprised look on her face. Then she shook her head with anger as if to say, *He has some nerve to threaten me.*

Wheeling, she lashed out with both hind feet. Tail tucked, Pirate stepped just out of reach, then spun and

150

bit Image on the rear, sinking his teeth into her glossy hide.

Melanie gasped. Furious, the filly charged Pirate, her front legs striking the air as if she were a wild stallion. Pirate dodged her hooves, spun, and kicked her hard in the ribs.

Image was thrown backward. When she regained her balance, she stood for a moment in shocked amazement. Ears flicking, she stared at Pirate, but Pirate ignored her and went back to eating grass.

On stiff legs, Image approached him. He reached around with his head and they touched noses. With a shrill squeal, Image struck out with one hoof, as if challenging him to fight. Pirate laid back his ears, swung his hindquarters around, and swished his tail.

Image backed away.

Melanie let out her breath.

"That didn't take long," Joe said.

"Thank goodness," Dani exclaimed. "I was about to rush in and protect Pirate."

"And I was about to rush in and get Image," Melanie said.

Lowering his head, Pirate started to graze again as if nothing had happened. Image nibbled at a blade of grass, her eyes watching his every move. When he ambled over to get a drink from her water trough, she followed. When he inspected her feed bucket, Image arched her neck and puffed up. For a second Melanie thought she was going to try to chase Pirate off, but when he turned, she scooted out of his way.

"Well, Melanie." Fredericka patted her hand. "I think your plan may work. My princess has met her match."

"It will work only if she starts respecting humans as much as she respects Pirate," Melanie said.

Joe clapped her on the shoulder. "You can teach her, Mel."

Melanie hoped Joe was right.

Later that night Melanie found Ashleigh working in the office. After telling her about Image and Pirate, she thanked her aunt.

"For what?"

"For reminding me why I started working with Image in the first place," Melanie said. "And also to tell you that I've decided not to go to New York."

When Ashleigh's lips parted in surprise, Melanie quickly explained. "I've been thinking about it all week, and I'd rather stay and work with Image. I'll miss seeing Christina ride at Belmont, but right now Image is too important."

Ashleigh grinned. "Of all people, I guess I should understand. But Susan and your dad are going to be really disappointed."

"I'll call him right now and explain," Melanie said, heading to the phone.

"You're not coming!" Will Graham exclaimed a few minutes later. "But honey, we haven't seen you in ages."

"I know, Dad, but this is a bad time. I've got a big test next Friday that I shouldn't miss," she fibbed, knowing that schoolwork came first with her father. "And I'm working with this special horse."

"A horse is more special than your dad?" Her father sounded like a disappointed ten-year-old.

Melanie laughed. "No. That's why I thought maybe you could come here that weekend instead. We can have the house all to ourselves. It'll be a chance for us to be together."

There was no sound on the other end of the phone, so Melanie knew her father was seriously thinking about the idea. "It's fine with Aunt Ashleigh," she added—not quite truthfully, since she hadn't asked her aunt. But she knew Ashleigh would think it was a great plan, too.

"Let me talk with Susan," Will said.

"Can you just come alone?" Melanie pleaded. She liked her stepmother but also liked the idea of having her dad all to herself. They never had much time together.

"I'd like to introduce you to Image."

"I assume Image is a horse and not the name of your new boyfriend," her father teased.

"Yes, she's a horse," Melanie said, laughing. "And I know you're going to love her as much as I do!"

14

"PIRATE'S READY," KEVIN CALLED DOWN THE BARN AISLE to Melanie. It was Monday afternoon, over a week since they'd put Pirate in with Image. Since that day, the training sessions with Image had gone better than ever before.

That afternoon Kevin had gotten off the bus at Tall Oaks with Melanie. He was going to help her pony Image for the first time. The filly had made such fast strides in her training that Fredericka had agreed to this next step—a necessary step if they were ever going to get her used to the track.

"Image is ready, too." Melanie tightened the girth on the racing saddle, giving the filly a treat when she didn't kick out.

Pirate clopped down the aisle, Kevin hobbling beside the big horse. He wore an Ace bandage and his knee was still sore, but he was able to get around without crutches.

Image danced in place, happy to see Pirate. Unsnapping the crossties, Melanie led her outside, following Kevin and Pirate down to the pasture.

Kevin held Image while Melanie mounted Pirate. "Keep her head snug against your thigh at first," he said. "Then feed her a little slack."

Melanie nodded. She'd ponied lots of horses, and she knew Image had been ponied before, so she didn't think they'd have any problems. When she was all set, Kevin handed her the lead. She'd worn gloves just in case.

They walked around the pasture, then moved up into a trot. Image seemed to float beside Pirate, and soon Melanie was smiling with delight. "She likes it!" she called to Kevin, who was watching by the gate.

As they rounded the corner Melanie saw two people come out of the barn. But then Pirate broke into a rocking canter, and she turned her attention back to the horses. Side by side they cantered around the perimeter of the pasture until Melanie said, "Walk." Her work with Image and the voice commands had paid off. Both horses dropped to a walk. Image shook her head and pranced as if to say, *That was fun!* but she didn't try to break away.

Melanie looked back toward the barn. Fredericka and Vince Jones were coming down the hill. Vince was gesturing toward Image.

"She looks better," Melanie heard him say when he reached the pasture gate. "In fact, it looks as if Tall Oaks might just have another winner."

Hearing Vince's words, Melanie beamed at Kevin. They'd done it! Even Vince saw now that Image had what it took to be a racehorse.

"I'm heading to New York tomorrow to be with Gratis," Vince continued. "But next Monday I'll send Jake over. He and Alexis can start backing her. The sooner we get Image on the track the better."

Melanie's heart skipped a beat. Jake? Alexis? What was going on?

Vince and Fredericka started back up the hill. "Wait!" Melanie called. When Vince turned, she told him, "Kevin and I are training Image. We've worked really hard."

Vince gave her a nod of acknowledgment. "And you've done a good job. But now it's time for my crew to take over. We've got to get Image working on the track as soon as possible."

"But you can't rush her," Melanie argued. "You can't just stick some stranger on her. It'll ruin everything we've done. Fredericka, tell him."

"I'm sorry, Melanie, but Vince has trained all my horses," Fredericka said. "I trust him totally. You can continue to help with Image at the farm, but once she's moved to the track, she's in Vince's hands."

Something inside Melanie snapped. "You'd put her in the hands of the trainer who said she wouldn't amount to anything?" she retorted.

156

Vince's look was scathing. "Excuse me, young lady. You have done a nice job with Image. But if you ever cross me like that again, you'll never set foot near her."

Melanie pinched her lips shut, but her eyes blazed. She was the one who loved Image. She was the one who believed in her. They couldn't do this!

Fredericka looked as if she wanted to say something, but then she took Vince's elbow and walked with him up the hill. Melanie watched them go, her eyes drilling into their backs.

She was so blind with anger, she didn't notice that Kevin had taken Image's lead from her. "I'm sorry, Melanie," he said. "I know how you feel."

"Looks like both our dreams got stomped on," she said between clenched teeth.

"Mel, I know you're angry, just like I was. And you want to blame someone. But sometimes things just turn out to be different from how you wanted, and it's nobody's fault."

"I know, Kevin. But right now I think I deserve to feel a little angry." Swinging her leg over the saddle, Melanie jumped off Pirate.

Kevin didn't say anything else. Not that she blamed him. What was there to say? She knew Image wasn't her horse. She'd only been fooling herself, dreaming about riding the filly for the first time. Dreaming about being her jockey.

Stupid, stupid dreams.

• • •

"Does that mean you're coming to New York with us?" Christina asked that night. The two girls were sitting on Melanie's bed. When Melanie got home that afternoon she had run straight up to her room, shut the door, and stayed there until her cousin finally convinced her to let her in. Christina and Parker were supposed to be studying together, but Parker hadn't arrived yet.

Melanie shook her head. She was leaning against her headboard, her pillow clutched to her stomach. Her insides hurt so much she felt as if someone had punched her.

"No. My dad's already made plane reservations to come here. Besides, this will be my last week with Image. I want to spend as much time with her as I can."

"You know, it doesn't mean you'll never work with her again," Christina said. "Maybe Vince will make you her exercise rider."

Melanie snorted. "After I told him off?"

"Oh, right." Christina's expression turned as gloomy as Melanie's.

Melanie sighed. "Besides, riding her once in a while wouldn't be the same. Working every day with Image is what made our relationship special. Just imagine not being able to see Star every day."

"That would be horrible," Christina agreed. She plucked at Melanie's quilt. "You know, I haven't really

158

told this to anyone, but one of my dreams is to buy Brad's share of Star. I know it's crazy—after all his wins, Star is worth a lot more money than I'll ever have."

Melanie cocked her head, listening carefully.

"And as long as Star is winning, Brad won't sell him. But I'm still saving my money, because I never, *ever* want to give up the dream of having Star for my very own."

"You're serious?"

Christina nodded. "Even though it's pretty much an impossible dream."

"Nothing's impossible," Melanie replied. She threw the pillow off her stomach and sat forward. "I've got money saved up, too. From my race wins. Maybe I could do the same thing!"

Melanie's eyes began to glow, and the pain in her stomach disappeared. "I know I don't have enough money, but maybe Fredericka would take monthly payments. I'd make payments for the rest of my life if I had to. At least then I could bring Image to White-brook, where Vince Jones couldn't get his hands on her!"

Christina nodded enthusiastically. "Go for it. It's worth a try!" The two cousins slapped palms, and Melanie jumped out of bed. "I've got to go to Tall Oaks and talk to Fredericka. She has to know that I'm serious. Do you think Parker would take me?"

"Only if you'll let me go with you."

Melanie grinned. "Sure. I'll need all the support I can get."

"Melanie, I know how you feel about Image, but I couldn't sell her to you," Fredericka said as soon as Melanie told her of her plan. "You're only sixteen." The older woman was sitting in the middle of her antique sofa. Melanie was perched on the edge of a gold brocade wingback chair. She felt totally out of place in Fredericka's house, and when the older woman hadn't jumped at her offer to buy Image, she'd felt stupid for coming.

"And I don't think you have any idea how much Image is worth," Fredericka continued. "Even if she doesn't win on the track, she's very valuable as a broodmare—though Vince assures me now that he's going to make her into as great a racehorse as Gratis."

Momentary anger flared in Melanie's chest. Three weeks earlier Vince had ordered Image off the track. Now he was ready to make her a winner. Melanie wanted to tell Fredericka what she thought of the trainer, but she kept quiet.

"I know I'm only sixteen, and I don't have much money saved, but I could make payments, Fredericka," Melanie persisted. "I don't think you realize how much Image means to me. I don't want to lose her."

Fredericka smiled. "You've forgotten that I love and believe in Image, too. I want to see her succeed as much as you do."

Melanie dropped her gaze. "You're right. I guess I had forgotten." Shoulders slumped, Melanie stood. "Thank you for listening to me," she said before leaving.

"Melanie, wait."

Melanie looked over her shoulder at the older woman.

"I've turned down five hundred thousand dollars for Image," she said.

Melanie swallowed hard. "That's a lot of money." More than she had ever imagined.

"Then there are track fees and training fees. Thoroughbred racing is an expensive sport. Would you really be able to afford her?"

"Uh . . ." Melanie wanted to say yes, but she had to shake her head. When she'd rushed over to Tall Oaks, she'd been so fired up that she hadn't thought everything through.

"Melanie, I know you love Image. And I hope you will continue to work with her. Spend as much time with her as you can. And don't worry about Vince. I'll make sure that he understands that you can see Image whenever you want."

"Thanks, Fredericka," Melanie said, and left. At least she could still work with Image. But she knew that once the filly went to the track, Vince would take over her training, and no matter what Fredericka said, Vince would get his own way. Melanie was sure that Vince's way would not include her.

Parker's truck was parked in front of the house. When Melanie climbed in, neither Parker nor Christina said anything. They must have known by the look on Melanie's face that Fredericka had said no.

The whole way home Melanie stared blindly out the side window. Christina and Parker tried to draw her into the conversation, but they soon gave up. Melanie didn't want to talk about anything.

Five hundred thousand dollars. Even half that was way more money than she could ever come up with. Emotion had clouded her judgment. Loving Image wasn't enough. Melanie had been foolish even to think she could afford such an expensive dream.

"Bye!" Melanie waved as Mike, Ashleigh, and Christina drove off. It was late Thursday afternoon, and they were headed to the airport for an evening flight to New York. As Melanie watched them leave, her heart grew heavy. That night the house would be quiet and lonely. Fortunately, her dad was arriving Friday afternoon. Melanie was dying to take him to see Image. All week she and Kevin had worked hard with the filly. And Image had made such great progress that this Saturday Melanie planned to try to mount her. Image would be going to the track on Monday, but Melanie was determined to be the first on the filly's back. After that . . . who knew if she'd ever ride Image again?

Melanie pushed the depressing thought from her mind.

When the car completely disappeared from view, she blew out her breath, already feeling lonely. Then she brightened. It was still light outside, and she hadn't worked with Image after school because she'd wanted to say good-bye to Chris and her parents. But if she could catch a ride to Tall Oaks, she could still visit Image before it got dark.

Melanie trotted to the barn. Kevin was helping Ian unload some bags of grain into the feed room. He agreed to drive her to Tall Oaks.

When Kevin pulled up to Fredericka's barn, Alexis was just unbolting the ramp from the horse van. A man Melanie didn't recognize was in the driver's seat.

Alexis frowned when Melanie got out of the car. "What are you doing here? It's almost dark."

"I came over to see Image."

Alexis hesitated. "Well, I'm afraid you're too late." She glanced at the driver of the van.

"What do you mean, too late?" Melanie asked.

Just then a shrill neigh sounded from the inside of the van. Melanie's heart froze. *Image!*

"What's going on?" Melanie demanded. She grabbed Alexis's wrist. "Why is Image in the van?"

"Vince phoned and told me to take her to Turfway."

"But no one told me. Fredericka never said a word. Vince isn't even here! He's in New York!" Melanie's voice rose higher and higher until she was practically screaming. She ran to the door of the van and began fumbling at the latch. "Image, it's me. I'll get you out of there. We had all weekend. We had until Monday!"

Alexis pulled Melanie away from the van. "Melanie, give it up. Image isn't your horse."

"But Fredericka said I could work with her until Monday!" Out of the corner of her eye, Melanie saw Kevin get out of the car and come over to her, but she was too upset to say anything.

"The plans have changed," Alexis explained. "Vince made the decision to move Image to the track early. He wants her to get used to her new stall over the weekend so that he can start working with her when he gets back on Monday."

"But that's too soon! Image isn't ready!"

Alexis shook her head. "Melanie, Vince has trained Fredericka's horses for a long time. He's one of the top trainers in Kentucky. He knows what he's doing. Besides, Fredericka was in on the decision to send Image to the track."

"But that's not fair." A sob rose in Melanie's throat. "No one told me."

"Welcome to the real world," Alexis said, giving Kevin a wry look.

Melanie backed away from the van, and Kevin put his arm around her shoulder.

After making sure the latch was secure, Alexis hopped into the passenger side of the cab. The truck motor revved and sputtered. Kevin squeezed Melanie's shoulder tightly as the van backed up and turned down the drive.

The van stopped at the gate to let a car pass on the road. Image's anguished neigh filled the air, and Pirate's answering bellow rang from the pasture.

Tears streamed down Melanie's cheeks, and her chest heaved.

Gently Kevin turned Melanie toward him. Breaking down, she sobbed in his arms. "I'm sorry, Melanie," Kevin said, his voice barely a whisper.

Pulling back, Melanie dried her eyes. "No, *I'm* sorry. I didn't mean to get so hysterical. I know Image isn't my horse. I knew this had to happen sooner or later. I—I just hoped it would be later." She stumbled over the words. "I wanted to be the first one to ride her. I just wanted a little more time with her." Melanie sighed heavily, her heart heavy in her chest. "I wanted to say good-bye." Frozen in place, she stared down the driveway, wishing the van would magically turn around and come back.

"So what are you doing to do about it?" Kevin asked.

"About what?" Turning, Melanie looked at him.

"About Image?"

Melanie shrugged. "What can I do?"

Kevin arched one brow and crossed his arms over his chest, waiting.

Melanie bit her lip, her mind beginning to race.

Kevin was right. She *had* to do something. "Uh, Kevin, how would you like to take another little drive?"

"Let me guess—to Turfway, right?"

Melanie nodded. "Right. Maybe I *don't* have to say good-bye to Image," she said, smiling mischievously.

"That's the girl I know and love!" Taking her hand, Kevin led her to his car.

Melanie climbed into the passenger's seat, steeling herself for another fight. Maybe Vince Jones was the best trainer in the Kentucky. But when Fredericka returned from New York, Melanie would convince her that she, Melanie Graham, was the best trainer for Image.

"And Kevin, will you go as fast as you can?" Melanie asked as Kevin started up the car. "I want to be there when the van gets there."

Image would be looking for her.

Alice Leonhardt has been horse-crazy since she was five years old. Her first pony was a pinto named Ted. When she got older, she joined Pony Club and rode in shows and rallies. Now she just rides her Quarter Horse, April, for fun. The author of more than thirty books for children, she still finds time to take care of two horses, two cats, two dogs, and two children, as well as teach at a community college.